# "Are you mad?" Fliss gasped

"No, I don't think so," Leon replied levelly. "I want our marriage resumed."

Struggling against hysteria, she narrowed her eyes. He had used her before, and for some reason—he always had a reason—he wanted to do it again.

"Over my dead body," she said tersely, equaling his calm indifference but experiencing a sickening sensation inside when he countered.

"Over Gerald's bankruptcy, too? The closure of the factory? The loss of around five hundred jobs?"

He was walking toward her, and she was too stunned to move. She could see the cool dark gray depths of his eyes, the mocking twist of his hard wide mouth!

"Think about it, Felicity. You agree to resume our marriage, or the merger's off. And if that happens, Harlies, Gerald, the work force, you—can all rot!"

**DIANA HAMILTON** creates high-tension conflict that brings new life to traditional romance. Readers find her a welcome addition to the Harlequin romance series and look forward to more novels by this talented author.

## Books by Diana Hamilton

### HARLEQUIN PRESENTS

993—SONG IN A STRANGE LAND
1248—A SECURE MARRIAGE

### HARLEQUIN ROMANCE

2865—IMPULSIVE ATTRACTION
2959—PAINTED LADY
2979—THE WILD SIDE

# DIANA HAMILTON

# betrayal of love

Harlequin Books

TORONTO • NEW YORK • LONDON
AMSTERDAM • PARIS • SYDNEY • HAMBURG
STOCKHOLM • ATHENS • TOKYO • MILAN

Harlequin Presents first edition October 1990
ISBN 0-373-11305-6

Original hardcover edition published in 1989
by Mills & Boon Limited



Printed in U.S.A.

## CHAPTER ONE

THE phone rang while Fliss was in the shower. To her tired ears it sounded more than usually insistent. Muttering, jet lag dulling her normally sharp mind, she wrapped her curvaceous body in a thick blue towel and padded through the open bathroom door to the tiny hallway, where she snatched the offending receiver from its rest.

She could hear hot water gushing wastefully from the shower-head, and her soft mouth formed the word 'damn!' as she settled the ear-piece beneath the silky, wet strands of her long dark hair.

'Yes?' The monosyllable came out as a snap.

'Fliss—so you're home safely. Did everything go well?'

'Just fine, Gerald. Thanks.' Irritation washed out of her voice as she recognised her boss's warm, mild tones. During the four years she'd worked for him, Gerald and his wife Netta had become closer to her than her real parents had ever been. But Netta had died suddenly, six months ago, and it was Gerald who leaned on Fliss now, looked to her for the support and companionship that helped fill the lonely hours his adored wife's death had thrust into his life.

'Good. You made your peace, then?'

'Yes, I managed that.' Her long fingers curled more tightly around the receiver as she forced a smile into her voice. Gerald and Netta had known all about her unhappy family life. It had been Netta, only a few weeks before her death, who had suggested that Fliss made the trip to America to visit her father, his wife and her stepbrothers and stepsister. And she had made her peace with them, but also, more importantly, with herself. She had at last been able to come to terms with the fact that, although her father and his new family had neither loved nor wanted her, it didn't mean she was unlovable.

But it was too complicated to talk about now, over the phone, with the droplets of water chilling her golden skin.

With her free hand she clutched the towel more tightly around her, bunching it up between her generous breasts, and listened to the sudden diffidence in Gerald's voice as he told her, 'This is going to sound like an imposition, Fliss, but could you possibly have dinner with me this evening? I know you've just got off what must have been a horrendously long flight, and you won't feel like——'

'Hold it! I was planning on coming over, anyway,' she cut in, her voice gently reassuring. She had been away for four weeks, and he would have been miserable and lonely, missing Netta. He and his wife had admitted the insecure and unhappy girl she had been four years ago into their lives, treating her like the child they had never had, and she knew that Netta would have wanted her to help Gerald through his bereavement as best she could.

'Well, thank you, Fliss,' Gerald said gruffly, and then, his tone more businesslike, 'I can't go into too many details now, but you know Harlie's has been going downhill—I'd been letting things slide, get out of hand.'

Gerald didn't have to blame himself, Fliss thought sadly—although she knew that he would. As managing director and chairman of the board, he would hold himself responsible for Harlie's decline.

She had been promoted to sales manager just over a year ago, and she'd been able to improve on already satisfactory sales figures, taking immense pride in the knowledge that, although the product range from Harlie Domestic Appliances was small, it was the best on the market. And full order books meant the factory was kept at full stretch, the workers' jobs secure. But four months ago Gerald had appointed a market research guy—partly, she suspected, to ease her own workload. And although she'd liaised closely with Tim Ormond, sales had started to drop off drastically. It had been something she'd worried about, worked on, but she'd kept her concern to herself—mistakenly, perhaps. She hadn't wanted to worry Gerald, though she was beginning to have suspicions regarding Tim's integrity, and Tim's appointment had been Gerald's brain-child. But the death of his wife had left Gerald a shattered man, his ability to cope around nil.

'I was going to discuss the situation with you as soon as I got back,' she said softly, and he laughed without humour.

'Ditto. I didn't want to bring it up before you went on holiday. I wanted you to get to know your family again, not to worry about the business.'

'Then we'll have a working supper,' she told him, trying to lighten his gloom. She would dry her hair and dress in something warm—a sweater and trousers—because late July in England was cold this year. 'I'll be with you in an hour.'

'It's gone too far for a working supper, Fliss. It's out of our hands.' He sounded almost relieved now, and she pulled in her breath,

'What do you mean—out of our hands?'

'Just that. Things blew up the day after you left. It all started with some damning rumours in the Press regarding our insolvency. Share prices fell, and more rumours followed—worse, of course. I've spent the last three weeks in intensive negotiations with one of the big international electronics conglomerates. I've had accountants and financial whiz-kids crawling all over me for weeks. But at last a merger has been agreed to in principle——'

'A merger?' Fliss interrupted sharply. 'Whose idea was that?'

'Theirs. I was approached about four days after you left for the States.'

'I see.' Fliss could hardly believe she was hearing this. Was Harlie's, renowned for the quality of its products, to be swallowed by some faceless international conglomerate whose concern lay only in the size of its annual profits? Quality and meticulous after-sales service would go by the board in pursuit of higher profit margins and, what was worse, production outlay would be slashed, corners cut and cut again, the work force decimated, throwing men who'd worked for Harlie's all their lives on to the scrap-heap of unemployment. She knew how the big boys worked.

'Are you sure you're doing the right thing?' she asked, her voice tight.

'It's the only thing. A merger is the only way to keep going at all. The board agrees, and we're having an emergency shareholders' meeting as soon as we can set one up. I shall strongly recommend that the merger goes ahead. And, Fliss, trust me. The company's lawyer and I have been over the small print with a magnifying glass, and it all looks good. I want you to meet their chairman—he's dining with me informally this evening and I want you to hear what he has to say.'

Her long sapphire eyes narrowed with puzzled incomprehension. Gerald sounded confident enough, even enthusiastic over the proposed merger. He sounded almost like the man he had been before Netta's tragic death. Had the trauma of the past six months taken even more out of him than she had guessed? Was he happy to shrug off the responsibility of the manufacturing company his father had founded?

'Wear something pretty, Fliss, and be nice to the man,' his voice broke into her racing thoughts. 'I want him to be as impressed by you as I know you'll be by him.' He chuckled softly, telling her, 'I'll send a cab round for you in half an hour. You won't want to drive yourself after the sort of day you must have had.'

Her unpacking would have to wait, Fliss thought distractedly as she stepped over the suitcases she'd dropped in the hall on her return to the small flat that had been her home for three years. She raced to turn off the shower, her mind in turmoil. She couldn't believe things had happened so quickly, it was like a nightmare.

When she'd flown out to California a month ago in an attempt to finally lay the ghost of her growing-up years, Harlie's had been a small but prestigious name in the world of domestic appliances. Things had been shaky in the sales field, and there had been cash-flow problems, but she'd spent most of her holiday thinking up schemes which might stop the rot—the first of which was to have been a full investigation into Tim Ormond's activities. She had a file full of notes ready to put to Gerald.

But now, it seemed, he was determined to take the easy option—to sell out to some flash electronics empire that would care nothing for anything save a quick profit.

A frown puckered her high forehead as she wrenched open her wardrobe door and peered in. She had taken her most glamorous things on holiday, and they were crumpled, packed in her suitcases—in any case, she was not in the mood for dressing up to impress, as Gerald had put it, the man who proposed to swallow Harlie's, chew it up and spit it out in some unrecognisable, tarnished form.

She was too tired to make intelligent conversation, feeling too much antipathy to be even basically polite to the type of man she knew Gerald's guest would turn out to be—arrogant, superior, blasé, and probably paunchy and soft with high living.

In any case, he would be uninterested in the qualms of a mere sales manager of a firm already down on its uppers, and only interested in the firm itself because the financial advisers he'd sent in would have assured him that, with drastic cuts in quality and the labour force, Harlie's could line his already bulging pockets.

Fliss shivered suddenly, only now realising how cold she'd grown while talking on the phone. Pulling herself together, she grabbed a navy cotton shirt-waister and struggled into it. Nothing frivolous or yielding about this dress; she needed to be businesslike, sharp. And looking the part of an on-the-ball sales manager with her firm's best interests at heart might help her to act it out.

She felt tired and shivery as she buckled the matching belt around her small waist and brushed the long strands of her hair back from her face, securing the dark, shiny mass with tortoiseshell clips. She had a sensuous body, graceful, almost lush—which the navy dress went some way to hide, she felt—and rich, dark hair which tumbled heavily around her shoulders when released from the pins and clips that normally tamed its wildness. Her sexuality was wholly feminine, but understated now. It drew admiring glances wherever she went, but she had learned to ignore it because the effect she had on men didn't interest her in the least.

After her brief and disastrous relationship with Leon Draker, four years ago, she had learned how to manufacture the armour she needed, and she wore it with confidence. And now that she had at last come to terms with her miserable childhood—with what she had seen as her parents' betrayal, their lack of love—she was completely her own woman.

Even her tiredness was working for her now, she decided grimly. It would make her irritable during the evening ahead, and she was assured enough, now, to turn that irritability into incisiveness. The big man wouldn't have it all his own way, she thought with acid satisfaction as the double toot of a car horn in the quiet street outside warned her that her cab had arrived.

* * *

The house which Gerald and Netta Harlie had lived in for most of their nineteen years of married life was on the outskirts of the market town of Marton Clee, near to the main factory and office block. It was a solid, comfortable Victorian dwelling that had become a second home to Fliss. And now, as she mounted the two broad stone steps, the front door opened, spilling mellow golden light into the blue twilight.

'Hello, Corky!' Fliss's smile for Gerald's housekeeper was warm and genuine, and she savoured it on her lips because it would quite possibly be the last genuine smile she would be able to give this evening. Already she could feel her hackles rising at the thought of having to meet the odious big wheel Gerald was doubtless oiling right now with his best malt whisky.

Frustration at not being able to have a quiet hour with her boss before having to meet the smooth operator who probably swallowed up firms like Harlie's without even noticing made her mouth tighten, her heart pound heavily. She would have liked to be able to find out if Gerald was selling out because he was simply too emotionally and mentally exhausted to carry on, or whether he and his advisers genuinely believed that a merger was the only way of securing Harlie's future.

Murmuring polite but abstracted responses to Corky's questions about her stay in the States, and her admiring comments on the tan Fliss had acquired, she relinquished the white wool blazer she'd worn over the severe navy dress and walked on spiky heels over the immaculate expanse of burgundy Wilton broadloom.

'I'm relieved you're back, and that's the truth.' Corky was hard on her heels, keeping up her usual unstoppable flow of conversation. Elderly, built like a bolster, Emily Corkerdale had been at Grange House for over a decade. She had been housekeeper to Netta's father and, when he had died, Netta had taken her in. She now ran the house like clockwork, and thought she knew all there was to know about Harlie Domestic Appliances. Now she stated, 'Poor Mr Harlie has been so worried. Not about the merger—that's the best thing that could happen for us all—but because you were away when it all blew up. You're as good as one of the family to him, and he was afraid you would think he'd gone behind your back.'

With her hand on the porcelain knob on the gleaming mahogany door to the sitting-room, Fliss paused, her face muscles tightening as Corky, with a cheery instruction to 'Go along in', plodded away to the kitchen.

Fliss couldn't be sure a merger was the best thing. It had all happened so quickly. Too quickly? But she would have a better idea when she had taken the measure of the man whose deep-toned voice she could just about hear as a slow, drawling counterpoint to Gerald's quicker, lighter tones.

Gritting her even white teeth together, and tilting her mouth into a smile that was tight enough, cold enough, to feel painful, she pushed open the door and walked in.

The room was warm. A leaping fire supplemented the central heating, giving life to the subdued tones of moss green walls, white cornices, russet and grey upholstery. But Fliss was cold. She felt as though she had walked inside an icebox. And there was a buzzing in her ears, cutting out Gerald's warm words of greeting as he rose from his chair.

She didn't see him, she didn't hear him. All she could see was the powerfully drawn, mocking face of Leon Draker, the man who had been—so briefly and disastrously—her husband. And all she could hear was that terrifying buzzing sound, like a million giant spiders rubbing their hands together, gloatingly inviting her to step into some vast, dark web.

## CHAPTER TWO

'FLISS, meet Leon Draker, chairman of Draker Electronics. Leon, this is Felicity Soames, my sales manager.' Gerald's voice dropped slightly, becoming warmer, deeper. 'Fliss to her friends.'

'Felicity.' Cool, strong fingers reached out for hers, touching them only briefly, yet leaving an aftermath of fierce, unbearable sensation. She shuddered, staring at him with dark-eyed shock, her heart pumping, out of control. She had walked out of his life, away from the travesty of their marriage, hiding herself like a wounded animal because she had been afraid he would follow and take his revenge.

But he hadn't followed—hadn't even filed for divorce. He hadn't cared enough to do either. Four years had passed, and each year had made her feel safer because she was sure he had forgotten her, as she had almost forgotten him. Until now, when a capriciously cruel fate had engineered this confrontation.

Speechless, almost rigid with shock, she closed her eyes briefly as Gerald placed an arm around her shoulders. Almost convulsively, she moved closer to him, instinctively seeking his protection, the comfort of being close to someone who didn't despise her, or think her worthless.

But closing her eyes had been a mistake because, when she lifted tremulous lids, she found Leon Draker's hard steel-grey eyes on her. Mocking, unkind, cynical eyes.

Gerald moved away, his mind too caught up in his own concerns to pick up the atmosphere. 'Your usual, Fliss?' he asked, and mixed her a dry martini, just the way she liked it. She wondered crazily if Leon recalled that her untutored tastes had run to orange juice or the occasional sweet sherry during the time of their marriage.

But at least Leon didn't appear to consider it necessary to tell Gerald that they were married, and that was a relief, because her marriage was something she'd never talked about—not even to the Harlies.

Shock began to recede at last, leaving her shaking. Speech returned—nothing more than slightly inane remarks when Gerald drew her into the conversation, but it was a start.

She had moved closer to the fire, because the way she was shivering with the inner coldness that had gripped her ever since she'd walked into this room was a dead give-away. But she was beginning to get herself together, and she forced herself to look at him, to face the hateful reality of his presence here, because only by facing it could she hope to cope with it.

He had changed very little. There were a few threads of grey in the thick, night-dark hair, the planes of his authoritative, fascinatingly male face were a touch sharper, the incisive character lines a shade deeper. He was in his mid-thirties now, but the extra years had only served to imbue him with a more impregnable urbanity, an even deeper self-assurance that made him totally unassailable.

The old mockery was still in his eyes, but had sharpened into a cynicism she didn't remember from the past, and the charm of his smile had gone, lost in the straight, hard line of his mouth.

By the time Corky came to call them through for dinner Fliss was back in control—or thought she was. Leon, as she might have known, had taken this unlooked-for, unwanted confrontation in his stride. Not by a word from that severe, chiselled mouth, nor by a look from those cold, clever eyes had he betrayed their secret. To all outward appearances they might never have laid eyes on each other before. His interest in her was vague, coldly polite, as befitted a potentate from the world of big business when confronted with a mere sales manager of a failing enterprise. In his eyes she was a creature of negligible ability and no importance—if what she suspected was true, and he was laying the blame for Harlie's poor showing at her feet.

There was nothing in his attitude to hint that they had shared eight short weeks of married life—that they were, in fact, still man and wife.

She had to be grateful for that. It was what she wanted, wasn't it? So why the momentary and incomprehensible feeling of pique because of his total disclaimer of their relationship?

Aware now that the two men were waiting for her, she stood up quickly, unconsciously smoothing the crisp cotton of her dress over her voluptuous hips, the smile she had hurriedly pasted on for Gerald's benefit dying away as she noted the way Leon's narrowed eyes followed the idle movement of her hand.

Shakily, she made herself walk towards them, fixing her eyes on Gerald. He was looking more animated tonight than she'd seen him since Netta's death. In his mid-forties, he was still a good-looking man, but beside Leon's superior height and breadth, that lithe, lean elegance, that indefinable but unmistakable aura of presence and style, Gerald paled into insignificance.

'Felicity...' To her distress, Fliss felt Leon's palm on the small of her back as he ushered her through to the dining-room, effectively leaving the older man to trail behind. Feeling desperate, she bit down on her soft lower lip, ordering herself not to squirm away from his touch, not to give him a clue, no matter how small, to the fact that he could still affect her in any way at all. The warmth of his strong, long-fingered hand burned through thin fabric, the barrier too insubstantial to be effective, the sensation created that of skin on heated skin. It made her legs shake, her mouth go dry. She wanted to cry—or scream!

She took her place at the table thankfully, unfolding her napkin and placing it demurely over her lap. She had to get things in perspective, she thought, meeting those cold, dark eyes across the table and dismissing the cool contempt she saw there with a mental shrug.

Leon Draker might not have changed much in the last four years, but she had. She was light-years away from the shy, insecure, incredibly innocent eighteen-year-old he had married. And if he wanted to pretend they were total strangers, then that was the best thing that could happen. It was fine by her. Like him, their relationship was the last thing she wanted to acknowledge.

All she had to do was to get through this evening as best she could. And then another four years could well go by before she laid eyes on her husband again. Even if the merger did go through, he would hardly bother himself personally with what would probably amount to the least of his many subsidiaries.

As she forced herself to spoon up some of Corky's delicious home-made mushroom soup, Fliss watched him from beneath thick, secretive lashes. The last time she had seen him he had been making love to Edwina; Edwina of the glittering green eyes and elegant, casual grace.

Suddenly, her throat closed in a spasm of agony—agony she'd believed to be long forgotten—and her spoon clattered against the rim of her bowl. His eyes found hers, alight with taunting amusement—as if he could read her thoughts, as if her agony could still give him some kind of warped satisfaction . . .

Gerald was saying something—Fliss couldn't make out the words for the roaring of blood in her head—and Leon obviously wasn't listening to what his host was saying because he cut through the older man's observations, his dark gaze on Fliss.

'How do you view the prospect of a merger, Felicity?' His lean fingers idly crumbled a bread roll, and one eyebrow peaked in a pointedly derogatory arch.

'I'm reserving judgement, Mr Draker,' her voice bit out coldly. The girl he had married would have coloured to the roots of her hair had she been asked to give an opinion on anything of deeper significance than the weather. Not that her opinion had ever been sought, even on so mundane a topic.

And now, despite the way Gerald's head had risen sharply at the ice in her voice, was as good a time as any to let Draker know just how much she had changed.

'That is, until I know exactly what your intentions are,' she added tartly.

Now that she knew who headed the international conglomerate which was angling for Harlie's, her suspicious wariness had increased a thousand-fold. He was a devious devil, as she knew to her cost, his motives never clear cut and simple.

'I assure you, they're strictly honourable,' he countered smoothly, daring her to disagree, although he had to know that she, more than most, was well aware that he wouldn't recognise an honourable intention if it jumped up and bit him.

'Fliss has been away for four weeks.' Gerald was pouring claret while Corky carved slices of hot roast beef, and his placating smile warned Fliss to watch her tongue.

But if she'd felt any compunction to temper her acidity for Gerald's sake, it was forgotten when Leon commented patronisingly, 'I'd forgotten, Gerald. Your dynamic sales manager has been on extended leave, as I believe you told me.' Cool eyes appraised Fliss's hectic cheeks. 'Had a lovely, lazy time, did you?'

'Very, thank you.' She was not going to rise, nor would she explain that her American holiday had been the only leave she'd taken in the past two years. Let him think she spent more time out of her office than in it. His opinion didn't matter a damn to her now.

She accepted the plate of meat Corky handed to her, seeing it as one more hurdle to be passed. The evening wasn't endless, even if it appeared to be. Another couple of hours should see it finished. And in the meantime she could still use the time to good advantage, ask a few pertinent questions, and maybe allow Gerald to see that having anything to do with this hard-eyed, soulless man had to be bad news where everyone connected with Harlie's was concerned.

'And how do you see the merger affecting Harlie's, Mr Draker?' She lifted her wine-glass and sipped sparingly. She needed to keep a clear head. Even now she could see the pinpricks of amusement in his cynical eyes, the tight line of his mouth, and she knew he would make a fool of her if he could. His mother had been an expert at doing that, at putting her timid young daughter-in-law in her place. He must have inherited that capacity, because no one could have bettered that *coup de grâce*, the hatefulness she'd walked in on, the final, exacting humiliation that had sent her scuttling away to hide like a broken, hurt animal.

'Not adversely, I hope.' It was the pat answer, the smooth reply that told exactly nothing. He was a past master at that, too, and her fingers shook with barely suppressed rage as she cut into her beef.

'You only "hope"? Is that good enough?'

Her teeth met with a snap, and Gerald, feeling—but far from understanding—the tension that almost made the very air twang, put in quickly, 'I think you ought to hear Leon's plans, Fliss, before you bite the hand that's going to feed you!' He laughed thinly, trying to make a joke of it, but Fliss cringed inside because she knew that it was no joke to him, it was deadly serious. He really believed Leon Draker was some kind of saviour. And he wasn't. He was a destroyer.

'Really?' Her throat tightened. She couldn't eat another thing.

'Yes, really.' Gerald gave her a warm, private smile, confident that once she had heard the details she would be as enthusiastic as he. He reapplied himself to his food; he was a meat and gravy man, always had been, even though Netta had done her best to introduce him to lighter, more interesting food.

'There's to be a huge injection of capital, for a start,' he told her around a mouthful of Yorkshire pudding. 'New plant and larger, more up-to-date factory premises. A massive advertising campaign to be run in all the quality mags—all the things we knew we should have done but could never afford.'

'And the quality of the product?' Fliss shot Leon a cold look. 'Harlie's has a reputation to maintain. Will we be able to achieve present standards if the labour-saving, corner-cutting methods of those who require a quick profit are used? Not to mention the built-in obsolescence which some manufacturers insist on to ensure the customers have to buy again in a couple of years' time? We don't manufacture for the throw-away market. And what about the workforce, Mr Draker?'

Fliss was beyond caring whether or not she was making Gerald squirm. It might hurt, but it might also open his eyes, make him think again about the advisability of entrusting Harlie's future to this...this predator!

'Do you intend to cut manpower in order to reach the required level of profitability?' she asked pithily. It was a subject close to her heart. During her time at Harlie's she had come to know most of her fellow employees—from the men in middle years who had worked in the factory or stores since leaving school to the youngsters just out of school, grateful to have a job. Gerald employed five hundred people, bringing a measure of security and prosperity to the small town. To have half, or more, of the workforce thrown on the scrap-heap would be a blow that would severely depress the area.

'Fliss!' Gerald broke into her heated diatribe, his hazel eyes anxious, but Leon raised a suppressing hand as if to say—'Leave her to me, I'll settle the brat!'

And that small gesture made her mad enough to forget any semblance of manners. It wasn't enough that he had ruined her life, he had to ruin the lives of scores, possibly hundreds, of hard-working people, too.

'Well, Mr Draker,' she stressed his name insultingly. 'May we have your projections of quality and manpower?'

'Certainly.' His smile was faintly pitying. 'Harlie's will continue to produce the Rolls-Royce models of the domestic appliance world. In fact, I shall expect the quality of design and function to improve. The whole of our vast research department will be on tap, leading, hopefully, to badly needed innovations. Harlie's products are good, very good, but even the best need updating. And as for the workforce,' he was beginning to sound bored, 'we shall eventually increase it, build a more up-to-date factory, and new housing for the influx of extra employees. I do hope,' he ended with a smooth smile, 'that your mind is more at ease.'

The devil was suave, no doubt about that, Fliss thought. But she didn't trust him an inch. She had very good reason not to. He had smooth-talked and charmed her into falling in love with him, fathoms deep in love, and had persuaded her to agree to marry him after only a few delirious weeks of knowing him. She had believed his suave declarations of love, only to find out, when it was far too late, that he had never loved her at all—that he had used her and their cruel farce of a marriage to punish the one woman in the world he had ever loved. Leon Draker was nothing but a heartless, sadistic egomaniac!

But Fliss was older now, wiser; wise enough to know when to hold her tongue. It would be better to talk to Gerald on his own, tomorrow. And in the meantime there was coffee to sit through, back in the sitting-room. She got through it somehow, even took part in the small talk, led by Gerald, until, grasping at a lull in the conversation, she stood up, her smile stiff.

'May I call a cab, Gerald?' Her deep sapphire eyes mutely apologised to him, but her excuse was valid. 'It's been a long day.'

The travelling had been bad enough, the drive back from the airport wearying enough to make anyone crave an early night. And that didn't take into account the trauma of coming face to face with Leon again, after four long years of trying to erase all trace of him, and of what he had done to her, from her memory.

She couldn't wait to get back to the privacy of her own small flat, to end an evening that had been doubly painful. Hearing of the proposed merger had been bad enough; seeing Leon again had been infinitely worse!

And something of the anguish she'd been trying so hard to hide must have shown in the depths of her vivid, black-fringed eyes because Gerald was on his feet at once, his kind, attractive features concerned.

'Of course. But you stay right where you are. I'll phone for you, or——' He hesitated, already on his way to the door. 'I could drive you back myself.' His eyes flickered uncertainly, torn between his desire to look after Fliss, who had become like a daughter to him over the past few years, and his duty as host to the most important guest he'd ever entertained.

'A cab will do fine,' Fliss assured him gently, understanding his hesitation, but the hatefully smooth voice of the man she'd hoped never to see again shattered her fragile equilibrium.

'There's no need to call a cab,' he said, and Fliss felt her head jerk round, as if pulled by an invisible string, and her mouth went dry as she encountered those mocking, slightly narrowed eyes and heard him add, 'It's time I made a move. I'll drop Felicity off on my way to my hotel.'

'No, thanks.' He'd been speaking to Gerald, but Fliss answered, and the scornfully delivered words popped out before she had had time to think about them. 'I wouldn't want to put you to any trouble. It's probably miles out of your way.'

If he was using the only decent hotel in town then he'd have to pass her door, but he wasn't to know that. For all he knew she could live ten miles out of town, in the opposite direction.

'It won't be any trouble, and I insist.' He was already on his feet: tall, wide shoulders which tapered to a narrow waist and hips, a lean, lithe body, totally masculine, unconsciously elegant in a perfectly tailored dark suit that must have cost a small fortune. He looked exactly what he was: a highly intelligent top-class tycoon, world-wise, an achiever, a man with whom no one, but no one, ever argued. Fliss had certainly never dared to argue with him, and not even his mother, the acid-tongued, redoubtable Annabel Draker, had attempted to openly dissent about his choice of bride. She had kept her mean-spirited tirades for Fliss's ears alone, leaving her in no doubt that she believed her beloved and exalted son must have suffered a brainstorm when he'd proposed marriage to such a plebeian, mouse-like nothing!

But he hadn't suffered any such thing, of course. He had known precisely what he was doing and why he was doing it. His motives had been of the nastiest when he'd asked the eighteen-year-old Fliss to be his wife. And she, made stupid with her consuming love for him, hadn't had the wits to question those motives.

Gerald wasn't arguing, either. He simply smiled, and said, 'That's good of you, Draker,' but Fliss wasn't eighteen years old and besotted any more. Fliss was giving as good as she got.

'I really would prefer a cab.' She walked to the door, her head high. Feeling the swish of cotton against her legs, she regretted not having dressed up. The navy shirtwaister had been an impulse buy in a summer sale. A mistake. It did nothing for her whatsoever. If she had worn one of her more sophisticated dresses, then he would have seen her, just for this once, as the woman she had become—coolly controlled, elegant—and not as an older version of the gauche creature she had been when he had married her.

She was already lifting the receiver of the phone in the hall, determined to call her own cab, when Gerald's hand closed over hers. Annoyed, she turned quickly, then bit down on a corner of her lower lip when she saw his anxious eyes.

'I know you've got to be exhausted, Fliss, and I blame myself for insisting you join us this evening. But try to be gracious, for my sake?' His hand tightened eloquently on hers, and the receiver dropped back on its rest with a tiny clatter. 'The man only offered to drop you off. He's not going to eat you. I don't want anyone or anything to rock this deal. If the merger doesn't go ahead, Harlie's is finished.'

She felt like a louse. She knew how her uncharacteristic behaviour must be upsetting him, and she dropped her eyes, the long lashes fanning her cheeks. She moved instinctively closer to him because she was sorry, he deserved better from her. And with Gerald she felt safe, even though she knew neither of them could ever breathe easily with Leon Draker around.

'I am sorry,' she murmured huskily, and, just for a moment, he held her close, his gesture affectionate, like a father comforting a troubled child. His voice dropped to a whisper.

'Don't antagonise him, Fliss. We need him.'

Like a hole in the head, she thought drily, then cringed as she heard the hated voice, almost purring, yet deadly.

'Ready, Felicity?'

'I suppose so.' And that was as gracious as she was going to get. She offered Gerald a weak smile and drew away from the comforting protection of his arms, moving over to the hall cupboard where she knew Corky had hung her blazer.

'I'll bring the car round.' Leon turned to Gerald, his eyes narrowing as he held out his hand, his mouth compressed in a bitter line that Fliss was at a loss to understand. 'It's been a rewarding evening, Harlie. I'll be in touch.' His mouth had a twist Fliss didn't like, and she knew he hadn't been referring to any business talk they might have had.

Expressionlessly, she watched him walk out of the door, remote, powerful, coldly assured in his persona of the head of an international conglomerate whose subsidiary companies were world-wide, whose wealth was incalculable.

Gerald helped her into her blazer, settling it round her shoulders like a child dressing a doll. When he had been talking to Leon he had looked like a fawning dog, she thought with distaste, though she couldn't blame him for being overly impressed by the man who could make others feel twitchy just by fixing them with those coldly authoritative eyes.

'Now, you won't bite his head off, will you?' he pleaded, following heavily behind her as she made for the door. She could already hear the impatient growl of a car engine on the drive outside, and for some reason the sound made her feel terrified—more nervously apprehensive than she had felt all evening.

'The journey won't take more than five minutes,' Gerald said, his voice strained as he strove for jocularity and, with the door open, she stood on the top step and looked back at him. Seeing Leon again had been a shock of the worst possible kind, and even five seconds alone with him was more than she felt she could take. Weary anger made her voice crisp.

'I don't think he'll pull out of a merger just because a mere sales manager—and a failed one at that—was a little less than grovelly, do you?'

She would have gone then, because the sleek black Porsche was already waiting, but Gerald snatched at her hand.

'Fliss, cool it. I'll talk to you tomorrow. Just don't say anything to annoy the guy. For my sake—if not for the firm's.'

Reluctantly, her eyes softened. Gerald and Netta had always been so good to her, and now that his much-loved wife was dead, and his company sliding down into insolvency, she couldn't turn round and poke him in the eye. She wasn't that kind of a heel.

She wished she could have told him exactly why she'd been less than polite to his guest, but it was a subject she didn't even want to think of herself, much less discuss with someone else—even someone as dear to her as Gerald. Thoughts of her brief and traumatic married life with Leon Draker were something she never permitted inside her head—although they did sometimes give her nightmares. She had never told anyone she was married, and now, with Leon waiting, was hardly the time to spring the news on Gerald.

'I won't say a word out of turn,' she promised ambiguously, then, clutching her blazer lapels together like armour, she walked quickly to the growling Porsche, her heart pounding. Whatever his reasons for keeping quiet about their relationship in front of Gerald, they would be no longer valid when she was alone with him in the dark interior of the car. The prospect of spending time alone with him made her feel ill.

Fliss got into the car, her legs shaking. She felt as if she were climbing into a tumbrel. But she gave herself a furious mental shake, compressing her soft mouth. He was still her husband, but there was nothing he could do to her now, no way he could reach her. He couldn't hurt her ever again. She was a different person.

'A touching farewell!' The bitingly acid comment was like a steel needle stabbing into her brain, and she sucked in her breath, gasping for air because his closeness in these confines was claustrophobic. 'Can't keep his hands off you, can he?'

Fliss said nothing, her teeth clamped together. She didn't have to justify her relationship with Gerald to him. Her life, and what she did with it, was her concern. He didn't own her—not any more. He had forfeited his rights when he had taken Edwina to his bed.

But he ignored her silence, his voice slightly patronising as he remarked, 'You changed your name. I prefer Felicity Draker to Fliss Soames.'

'Really?' She couldn't care less what he preferred. She loathed him.

He had always called her Felicity, and she'd changed it to Fliss as soon as she'd been capable of thinking coherently after she'd walked out on him. It suited the image she had made herself cling to in those days—the image of the new self she had so desperately wanted to create. The name Felicity had always seemed so demure, so biddable, and Soames was her maiden name so she'd reverted to that because she hadn't wanted anything to remind her of her marriage. But he wouldn't remember her maiden name; she doubted if he remembered anything at all about her. She had been that unimportant to him.

They were pulling out on to the main road that led to the centre of Marton Clee, and she would give him directions to the opposite side of town from where she lived. She was bone-weary, but she would rather walk miles than have him know where she lived.

'If you insist on driving me home,' she said stiffly, 'then turn left at the next crossroads and——'

'I know where you live.' He sounded amused, as if he enjoyed catching her out in a lie, and she jerked her head round and stared furiously out into the street-light-spattered darkness. She might have known!

'Gerald told you,' she stated at last, her lower lip protruding mutinously, her skin crawling as she heard his light, humourless chuckle.

'I didn't need to pry the information out of him. I've made it my business to know exactly what you were doing, where you were, for four years.'

She absorbed this information in sick silence. She didn't doubt he was speaking the truth. He knew how to get what he wanted—he always had done—and she should have taken that into account.

She moved uncomfortably in her seat as he drew up at traffic-lights, tapping the steering-wheel with the pads of his fingers as he waited for green to show. This journey already seemed the longest she had ever taken. Her nerves were on edge, jangling intolerably. She could have passed the time by asking why he'd kept tabs on a wife he'd never wanted, but she didn't want the added contact of speech.

He certainly hadn't been kept informed of her movements because he was interested, or concerned. Interest and concern hadn't had any part in their relationship—not on his side. She couldn't believe those qualities had suddenly manifested themselves after she'd left him. And he hadn't wanted a divorce, or he would have started proceedings years ago.

So Edwina must be unavailable. She must have married someone else—or died. That thought made her shudder. According to the way Edwina had told it, she and Leon had shared a love that went back years, that would survive even beyond death.

'Cold?' The enquiry set her teeth on edge. What did he care? And she lifted her shoulders in a careless shrug, not bothering to answer, certainly not willing to tell him of the dark thought that had caused her to shudder so violently.

He drew up in front of the house where she lived, cutting the engine, and she sat staring blindly into the darkness, punch-drunk from tiredness and the events of the evening, until the passing headlights of a car made her blink, bringing her back to reality. The nightmare was over at last.

The dreadful evening was at an end. He had delivered her home and their short, unpleasant reunion was over. Scrabbling, she unclipped her seat-belt, opened the door and almost fell out on to the street in her flurry to get away.

Running blindly around the front of the car, she gasped with distress when she realised he'd reached the front door before her. Standing, feeling stupid and inept, she stared at the dark bulk of his body outlined against the ghostly white paintwork. He held out a hand, his voice goading her.

'Give me your key.'

'Get lost!' She was not his property to be ordered around, told what to do. Not any more. And her voice was frigid; the icy contempt would have frozen off any other man. But not this one.

'Felicity,' he sounded bored, 'I'm coming in. We need to talk. Either you accept that, or I make one hell of a scene right here on the street. It's your choice.'

If the devil himself had issued an ultimatum, it couldn't have been worse. She could already see the curtains at the ground-floor flat window twitching, revealing a sliver of light. Miss Pargeter lived alone with her cat, and she enjoyed nothing better than to gossip with the neighbours. A good piece of news guaranteed her entry through a dozen front doors, with coffee and biscuits thrown in if she got her timing right. It was a way of easing her loneliness.

Fliss liked to keep a low profile, and what Miss P would gleefully relay to all and sundry if Leon carried out his threat to create a scene on the doorstep didn't bear contemplating. It made her brain ache just thinking about it.

So she moved stiffly along the short garden path, already fumbling in her bag for the door key. Having Leon invade the privacy of her home wasn't appealing, but it couldn't be helped. All she had to do was to remember that he couldn't hurt her any more. She had stopped loving him four years ago.

And he assuredly wouldn't claim his conjugal rights, she thought cynically. The marriage had been less than a week old when he'd made it plain he didn't want her in his bed. She had been too young, too naïve and inexperienced to satisfy him. She had known that, or at least feared the possibility of it, before the marriage, and the confirmation of her fears had torn her apart, killing the small amount of self-confidence she did have at that time.

Perhaps they did need to talk, she thought tiredly as she watched him pick his way around the suitcases she'd abandoned earlier, making with uncanny instinct for her sitting-room.

She had lived here for just over three years. When she'd first gone to work for Harlie's, as secretary to the then sales manager, she had roomed in a dismal bedsit. When she'd met Netta at her first company Christmas party, they had taken an immediate and instinctive liking to each other. Netta had been a comfortable, motherly lady, and had taken the shy, defensive Fliss under her wing.

It had been Netta who had persuaded her to find better accommodation, and they had flat-hunted together. Though, over lunch in town one Saturday, after a particularly abortive session, Netta had said, 'I've been thinking Fliss. Gerald and I are both very fond of you—in fact, he's told me he's never had such a promising new employee, and he's very proud of the way you take all those evening business courses. But I can't help worrying—if I'd been lucky enough to have a daughter, I'd have been worried sick if she worked the hours you do. When, I ask myself, do you take time to make yourself a proper meal? No, don't answer that!' She'd smiled at Fliss's wry expression. 'I don't think I could bear to hear it! But, seriously, why don't you come to Gerald and me? Grange House is too big for us, you'd help fill it, and, before you say anything, I've talked it over with Gerald and he's all for it. He already sees you as his new sales manager when Patterson retires, and, more than that, he's beginning to look on you as a kind of daughter—as I have for months now.'

It had been a kind offer, and one that had been repeated at intervals, but although Fliss had grown deeply fond of her boss and his wife, and had spent many a happy evening in their company over one of Corky's excellent meals, she had preferred her independence, her own space.

Now, seeing Leon in her sitting-room, casting no doubt disdainful eyes over her carefully chosen bits and pieces, she knew that her space had been defiled. It had always been her refuge, her private world, the first place she had been able to call a real home. It would never feel the same again.

'Nice.' His voice was dry, damning with faint praise. He probably thought the place was appalling. Feathergay was a small mansion, and he'd been brought up like a prince, surrounded by fine antiques, superb paintings. And the view from the mullioned windows embraced delightful formal gardens, rolling parkland and gentle Somerset countryside, not a narrow, small town street.

'We'll have coffee, shall we?' He had already switched on the electric fire and was standing in front of it as if he had rights. It annoyed her intensely.

'Just say what you have to say, and go.' She wouldn't give him anything, not even coffee. Four years ago he had taken everything she had—her happiness, her self-respect, her innocence. She had nothing left for any man, let alone him.

He shrugged slightly, his powerful shoulders lifting minimally beneath the smooth, expensive suiting, his austerely handsome face devoid of expression,

'As you like. I had hoped we might make this meeting a little more relaxed. But have it your way.' Slowly, his eyes drifted over her, assessing eyes that betrayed not a flicker of warmth. But her skin burned where those dark eyes touched. Her body was aflame beneath the prim navy dress and severely styled blazer.

'What do you want?' Her mouth was dry. 'A divorce?' She began to shiver, although she wasn't cold. He had forgotten her for four years, but had been unexpectedly thrown into her company tonight, and that had reminded him that he had a wife—a wife he had never wanted. So he had now decided to use the law to be finally rid of her, to tidy things up, and it would be the best thing for both of them. 'I've no objections, and I won't ask for alimony—if that's what has been holding you back. I wouldn't touch a penny of yours if I were starving,' she stated icily, maintaining total control even though he was still touching her with his eyes, his glance caressing her lips, breasts, thighs, making comparisons, maybe, between her opulent curves—his mother had called her figure 'common'—and the elegantly sophisticated, thoroughbred lines of the type of women who would populate his life. Women like Edwina.

'Not a divorce.' He had moved away from the fire and picked up a white porcelain cat. She'd bought it from a car-boot sale, and it was decorated with tiny blue flowers and was probably early Victorian. She would never feel the same about it again, not now he had held it between his hands.

'What, then?' she snapped at the back of his smooth, dark head. She hadn't moved further into the room, and she wouldn't—not while he was here. 'Well?' she prompted acidly, wanting him out. The sooner he said what was on his mind, the sooner he would go. And if it wasn't divorce, then she couldn't imagine what he could want to discuss with her.

'I want our marriage resumed,' he told her levelly, with no more emotion than if he'd been asking for a packet of tea over a shop counter.

Fliss gasped, her stomach contracting sickeningly, and her voice was rough as she grated, 'Are you mad?'

'No, I don't think so.' He was looking at her now, still holding the porcelain cat, his face blank. Crazily, she wished the cat would come to life, bite him—anything to shake him out of this effortless control, this icy indifference.

Struggling against hysteria, she narrowed her eyes. She was no longer a silly, love-struck girl; she was an intelligent woman. He had used her before, and for some reason—he always had reasons—he wanted to use her again.

'Over my dead body,' she said tersely, equalling his calm indifference, but experiencing a sickening sensation inside when he countered,

'Over Gerald's bankruptcy, too? The closure of the factory? The loss of around five hundred jobs?' He had replaced the ornament on the table and was walking towards her, and she was too stunned to move. He was close now, too close, and her wide sapphire eyes tilted, riveted to those austere features, seeing the flecks of pure silver in the cool, dark grey depths of his eyes, seeing the mocking twist of the hard, wide mouth. 'Think about it, Felicity, because that's what it comes down to. You agree to resume our marriage, or the merger's off. And if that happens, Harlie's, Gerald, the workforce, you—can all rot.'

'You can't mean that!' She had stood her ground through this nightmare, not moving from her stance near the door, but her mind was whirling in a maelstrom of bitter disgust, and now she felt near collapse.

'Utterly.' He touched her, moving her gently out of his way, and she almost disintegrated beneath the welter of unwelcome sensation his hands sparked through her cringing flesh.

But his hand was on the door now, and he turned, his smile cool, terrifying.

'I've given you my ultimatum, and now I'm giving you time to think it over. I'll pick you up here tomorrow evening—sevenish. We'll have dinner, and you can tell me what you've decided.' He smiled thinly, the coldness of his eyes underlining his parting words, 'And don't make the mistake of thinking I'm not serious. I've never been more serious in my life.'

## CHAPTER THREE

Fliss leapt out of her geriatric Mini and bounded up the steps, pressing her finger hard on the brass doorbell. She hadn't slept, and it showed, but she'd done her best with heavier than normal make-up, and had chosen a blouse in a jaunty shade of yellow to wear with the newest of the sleek grey suits she favoured for office wear.

But tendrils of glossy dark hair were already escaping from her chignon, normal severity being impaired by fingers that had refused to stop shaking.

The hall clock was striking eight as Corky opened the door, not in the least surprised by this early visitation, because Fliss had often joined Netta and Gerald for breakfast if there had been business matters to discuss informally and, latterly, to give Gerald support and the feeling that he was not alone in the bleak months since Netta's death.

'Eggs?' Corky lifted an enquiring eyebrow. 'Or I could do you a kipper in next to no time.'

'Just coffee, thanks.' Fliss didn't think she would ever eat again, and this morning it was she who was looking for comfort. If Gerald told her that Leon Draker was the answer to a prayer right now, but they'd manage without him if they had to, then she, Fliss, would be one mightily relieved lady and could tell her husband to go and jump in a lake.

She scurried to the small breakfast-room at the end of the passage, her high heels clicking on the parquet;

she was as edgy as a cat. Gerald looked up from his kipper, and Fliss winced, because this morning he looked his age.

Last night, when she'd arrived for dinner, he'd looked like a man who'd had a load lifted from his mind. But by the time she'd left he'd looked nearly desperate. She hated to think that her behaviour had been responsible for the change. She owed him so much.

'I'm glad you came.' His smile was tired as she slipped into the chair opposite his. 'I was going to phone you before I left for the office.'

She nodded tersely. This was no time for caginess. 'How important is this merger to Harlie's?'

'It's vital.' He glanced across the room, frowning as Corky came in with an extra cup and a fresh pot of coffee, and his grunt of thanks was dismissive, making Corky sniff as she plodded out again, her nose in the air. 'I won't be fit to live with until the deal's gone through,' he said wryly. 'You've no idea what it's been like these past few weeks—the rumours, the fall in share prices...'

Sales had been dropping off for months, Fliss knew that—who better? Again she wished she'd emphasised the falling figures to her boss, told him of her concern, instead of glossing them over, afraid to add more to the burden he already carried. His ability to cope with day-to-day problems had been severely curtailed since Netta's death.

'If a merger of some sort is really necessary, couldn't we look elsewhere?' She wasn't a member of the board, although she had had hopes in that direction. At the moment she was merely the sales manager—and not a very good one, it seemed, she thought wryly.

Gerald had always listened to what she had to say, valued her opinions. But not now, though.

'Out of the question. There are few consortiums large enough to give us the boost we need, and none who would offer what Draker's put on the table.' He buttered a slice of toast, his mouth lifting in an enquiring smile that did nothing to erase the worry from his eyes. 'What have you got against the man, Fliss? It's not like you to take an immediate dislike to someone, and even less like you to let it show. Oh, I realise you must have been bushed out of your mind last night, and I wouldn't have asked you to join us, but Draker insisted. You were the only member of the managerial staff he hadn't met.'

Fliss grappled with the implications of that as she made drinking her coffee her excuse for a few moments' silence. On his own admission Leon had kept tabs on her, had known exactly where she was and what she was doing, therefore he would have known her position in the company, and their meeting last night would have come as no shock to him. He had insisted on her joining them for dinner. So his diabolical plan to insist on her agreeing to resume their marriage must have been festering in his mind for some time. It was far more frightening than if it had been a spur-of-the-moment decision. And had he somehow engineered Harlie's into their present unenviable position? She could hardly believe that. He was capable of such a devious move, but why would he waste so much time and effort on placing her in a position of weakness? He had never wanted her—she had been simply a means to an end and she had served her purpose. It didn't make sense.

She replaced her cup on its saucer, avoiding Gerald's eyes. She could hardly answer his question by saying, 'I detest him because he once broke my heart, because he married me out of spite, to pay someone back, and he didn't give a damn about my feelings. And the only way this merger's going to go ahead is if I agree to resume the marriage I walked out on four years ago.'

She couldn't say that, because she had never told anyone about her ill-fated marriage—not even Netta, who had become the nearest thing to a mother she had ever had. She had always felt too ashamed to speak of it—ashamed of the incredibly gullible, love-starved, insecure creature she had been at eighteen. She cringed whenever she thought about that younger self.

So she said, 'I don't like his type. He's the sort who manipulates people, uses them.' And that was the truth, although Gerald would probably think she'd gone off her head. 'Has Draker Electronics been buying heavily into Harlie's stock recently?' Her voice was acid as the thought occurred, and her eyes narrowed at Gerald's shrug.

'Fairly heavily.'

'And selling?' She knew she was right, it was a gut reaction to what she knew about Leon's predatory instincts, to the growing fear that his reason for wanting her to take her place as his wife again was somehow important enough for him to have manipulated this situation.

'Recently, and heavily?' she persisted. 'Ensuring a lack of market confidence, a sharp drop in the price of shares? If that's not manipulation, I don't know what is.' She stood up, ready to go, to leave him with something to ponder over, but Gerald was at her side almost immediately,

'Fliss—are you annoyed because all this went through while you were away?'

'I have no right to be,' she said stiffly, buttoning her jacket with impatient fingers. If he thought that, then she had no real objections—at least he wouldn't be able to guess the truth.

'I thought you'd be happy to know that Harlie's has a future.' His moist, miserable eyes defeated her, and she managed a smile.

'Of course I'm glad. You must know that.'

Gerald didn't have anything to fear—as far as he knew, merging with Draker could only be good news. He must think her a spoiled, illogical brat, snapping at the hand that had helped her along the rough path through the business world.

'As long as you're satisfied,' she added then, falsely bright, knowing her own future would be ruined if the merger were to go ahead, yet unable to tell him so. And her reply pleased Gerald, who was collecting his briefcase.

'More than satisfied. Draker might have done some manipulating, but that's the way a lot of these big guys work. Oh, and Fliss, drop by my office later, and I'll let you have the relevant files on the Draker proposition.'

The files didn't make good reading—not to Fliss. No wonder Gerald and the rest of the board looked on Leon Draker as a knight in shining armour. Harlie's future couldn't have been painted in a rosier wash.

But Fliss was still fighting; her whole future was at stake. If she could somehow prove to Gerald that they could work their own way out of this mess, then there might be a slim chance that she, through Gerald, could persuade the rest of the board to forget the merger.

She worked non-stop through the morning, missing her lunch-break, phoning their retail outlets, checking through files, and when Penny, the secretary she shared with Tim Ormond, brought her a mug of tea at three-thirty, Fliss wiped a strand of hair from her forehead with the back of her hand and groaned.

'Thanks, love. I'm parched.'

Penny said, 'No wonder, scrabbling through that lot.' She wrinkled her nose at the scattered files. 'Drink your tea—oh, and have you heard about the merger? We're all over the moon at the prospect—and I'm over the moon about their big guy, Leon Draker! You should just see him, Fliss. Dishy just isn't the word! I'd do a personal merger with him any day of the week. I went weak at the knees just looking at him.'

'He came here?' Fliss lifted her nose from her mug, her eyes sharpening.

'Sure. Had a long interview with Tim, went through all the files. It's nice that the big guy takes such a personal interest, don't you think?' She touched one of the files on the floor with the toe of a spiky-heeled scarlet shoe. 'Want me to put these away?'

'What?' Fliss's sable brows met in a frown. 'No—yes, I mean. I can't seem to find the Martin and Bride file. Has Tim got it?'

'I think so.' Penny perched on the end of the desk, her tight skirt riding up towards her thighs. 'I'll check, shall I?'

Fliss nodded. 'Thanks. And ask him to get himself round here, I want to see him.'

'Still out, sorry.' Penny shook her head, her round pink mouth twitching because Tim Ormond was a charmer, albeit a lazy charmer. 'Another long, boozy lunch with a customer.'

Sapphire eyes hardened as Fliss decided to do something about that. Before Tim had taken the manufactured market research post Fliss had occasionally entertained customers. But her expense dockets had looked like peanuts compared with Tim's, and there hadn't been nearly so many of them.

She had been happy enough at first to leave the entertaining to Tim. She could deal with people, but preferred not to have to—a remnant of her early insecurity, she supposed. But she had warned Tim several times about his overspending, to no avail. This time she was going to have to be firmer. The trouble was, Gerald had created the position when, shortly after Netta's death, an old schoolfriend had turned up out of the blue, asking if Harlie's could offer his son a job. And Gerald, needing friends at that time and believing that Fliss had too great a workload, had gone against Fliss's advice. She hadn't needed a research assistant, and Harlie's couldn't afford one now.

'Anyway,' Penny was on her way to the door when she remembered to ask, 'how was the holiday? I bet your family was glad to see you after all this time.'

It had become common knowledge that Fliss's family had gone out to America several years ago. Fliss had been seventeen when her father had left the police force and had been offered a security job in California. What no one did know was that Fliss, in her first year of a secretarial course, had opted to stay behind because the invitation to go along had been less than half-hearted. Her family, such as it was, had never wanted her. And one thing her holiday in the States had done was to prove, finally and completely, that Fliss was her own woman, could stand on her own feet, and didn't need anyone.

Her father and stepmother were happy, and she was glad of that. Their children were part of a close family circle which didn't include her and never had. She could face that now. She could recognise that it wasn't her fault, and it didn't hurt, not any more. And she should be celebrating the demise of the last of her juvenile hang-ups, but right now she was in no mood to celebrate anything—not with Leon's ultimatum hanging over her head.

'It's an indifferent menu, but I can recommend the beef Chianti.' Leon passed her the leather-bound menu, and Fliss skimmed it with resentful eyes.

'I'll have the sole,' she said, out of sheer perversity. 'Have you been staying here long?' The Crown was the only decent hotel in Marton Clee, and the locals used the almost-sophisticated restaurant when they felt like living it up. But to Leon Draker it would be lacking in style, small-town, and he wasn't a small-town man.

'A few days. I return to London tomorrow.'

He might just as well have said he'd be returning to civilisation, she thought, her mouth tightening. Marton Clee might be a bit behind the times, its inhabitants small fry, but it was a good place to live.

She glanced across the table at him with hard, bright eyes. He was dressed immaculately, of course, in a perfectly tailored silver-grey lounge suit, his tie a subtle blend of greys and blues against the whiteness of his cambric shirt. He was the most compelling man in the room—that was an inescapable fact. He had presence and looks, a superb physique, and that indefinable something else that marked him out as a man of breeding. But she had never hated him as much as she hated him now. She hated him more now than she had when she'd walked in and found Edwina in his bed.

He had broken her heart then, reduced her to nothing. But she had been nothing much when he'd married her, an insecure child, so she hadn't had far to go before she'd reached rock-bottom. And from rock-bottom she'd clawed her way up. Her insecure childhood, her awful marriage, had made her highly motivated, determined to prove herself, because if she hadn't done that she would have been a nothing for the rest of her life.

And she had proved herself when Gerald had given her the chance, believed in her, and now Draker was knocking her back down to basics and this time there was further to fall.

Because, if he still insisted, she had no other option but to resume their marriage. One look at the Martin and Bride file had told her that. The chain of exclusive stores had represented their largest retail outlet, but three weeks ago they had declined to renew their contract, and without that contract Harlie's had no chance of pulling through on their own—not the way things were at the moment.

A quick phone call to the head buyer at Martin and Bride's had confirmed her worst suspicions: Tim Ormond had quoted terms and delivery dates and quantities that had put Harlie's products in the 'non-viable' drawer. Had Leon put the younger man up to it, seeing the loss of that contract as the final nail in Harlie's coffin?

Fliss sipped from the glass of white wine she'd asked for, agitatedly aware of Leon's smoky eyes. He was tricky, very tricky, because tonight his eyes held an echo of the humour that had attracted her so in the first place. Four years ago she had believed that look indicated warmth. Now she knew better. There was no warmth in him; the humour was mockery.

'We're not here to discuss my hotel accommodation, Felicity.' The lights in his eyes were brighter now, the quirk of his mouth bordering on a smile. Fliss shook off the untenable sensation of intimacy, of a softness in him that was almost gentleness. It was no such thing, merely a trick of the light, the guttering, fluttering light from the candle on the table between them.

She moved the candle slightly to one side so that she could see him as he really was, and not in a romantic, hazy glow. But that didn't help, because shadowed eyes say nothing.

'You've reached a decision?' His tone was markedly bland as a waiter came forward with their orders, and Fliss nodded tightly, not trusting herself to speak. He remarked, 'You don't look too pleased about it—whatever it is.'

'Should I be?' A flash of temper made her face feel tight, the skin tautly stretched over her bones. 'You barge back into my life, hurl threats around——'

'Threats?' He shook his head and began to cut into his beef. 'Hardly. I merely pointed out the advantages of the proposed merger.'

'So you did. You also said the merger was contingent on my agreeing to go back to you.' She scraped at the fish with her fork, admiring the steadiness of her hand with the part of her brain that was still capable of rational thought. Keeping cool was difficult. If she allowed herself to think of her past with him, or of their future, she would go to pieces. The only thing to do was to focus her mind on the here and now, on this precise moment of time when she was sitting opposite this man—the man who had been the target of all female eyes since they'd entered the restaurant.

Fliss smiled without humour. Every other woman in the room might be envying the curvaceous, raven-haired woman who was being wined and dined by the most attractive, charismatic male ever to breathe Marton Clee air. But how little they knew how unenviable her situation actually was!

'Eat your fish,' he commanded distantly, and Fliss stared down at the mess she'd made of the food on her plate, then pushed it impatiently aside. How could she swallow a thing when the words that would ruin the whole of her life were about to be forced from her?

When she flicked a glance across the table his stillness frightened her, set her heart pounding as if it might break free of her breast. There was a menace about the frozen immobility of his features that made the future seem suddenly terrifying.

'There are around five hundred jobs on the line here, Felicity,' he reminded her, his voice like silky steel. 'Not to mention plans for a large injection of much needed capital—not only to fund the new premises and plant, but research and development, too. Plus,' he put his cutlery down on his plate, 'the probable creation of up to two hundred new jobs. Are you willing to sacrifice all that?' His mouth twisted down in a bitter line. 'Am I such repulsive husband material? There was a time when you didn't think so.'

She flushed, annoyed with herself for the revealing stain of colour she could feel burning her face. Even now she could still remember how much in love she'd been, recall how the lightest touch of that sculpted male mouth against her quivering lips had been enough to set her on fire for him.

'I can't sacrifice Harlie's—and you know it.' She licked her tongue over her lips. 'It's just—just…' Her voice thickened and faltered. She was losing control because, damn him, he was making her feel like a gauche teenager again, unsure of herself, of her own worth, her own identity. And these were the things she was going to have to sacrifice if Harlie's were to remain in business.

'What are you trying to say, Felicity?'

'Don't tell me you can't imagine!' she ground out hollowly, snatching her empty wine-glass away from the bottle he held out over the table. Any more to drink and her inhibitions would fly out of the window, and she'd be telling him, loudly exactly what she thought of him!

'I just don't go a bundle on what I'm being asked to pay to keep the merger on the cards!' she hissed, just loud enough for him to hear, because she'd collected herself again, grabbed hold of her slipping poise with both hands.

'Pay?' There was a look of severe distaste about the severely moulded mouth. It was a look he had mastered well, she remembered with a shudder, recalling the time when he'd found her in tears of humiliation and, in answer to his softly concerned query, she'd begged him to take her away from Feathergay, explaining between sobs how his mother deliberately tried to make her feel a worthless wimp. That look of distaste had been in evidence then, replacing the manufactured concern as he'd told her, 'It's time you made an effort to grow up, to assert yourself, and accept your position here as my wife.'

But it didn't do to remember anything about those few weeks of married life, because once she started she probably wouldn't be able to forget again. First time round had been difficult enough. And part of her long battle with herself had been to banish memories of the way that mouth, now so hard and evincing such distaste, had felt against hers.

'As I recall, you weren't asked to *pay* anything.' His cool voice emphasised the inadvisedly chosen word. 'Merely to resume your duties as my wife. We are still married, Felicity.'

'That doesn't mean to say I like the situation.' Her lips moved in a mockery of a smile as the waiter appeared to remove their plates.

Offered the dessert menu, Leon declined with a slight, expressive movement of his dark head. 'My wife isn't hungry, I'm afraid. But we'll both have coffee.'

His reference to her as his wife brought agonised colour to her face. It brought reality too close to home. And, ignoring her discomfort, he took up her comment. 'If you wanted to change the situation, you could have gone for a divorce long ago. Why didn't you?'

'Because putting it in motion would have necessarily reminded me of you,' she bit out, 'and that I didn't want!'

Her hands were remarkably steady as she poured from the plated silver pot that had just appeared. She had given him the answer she had always given herself whenever her mind had been unguarded enough to allow thoughts of her marriage to enter her head.

'And why didn't *you* divorce *me*?' She was attacking now. 'It was a farce of a marriage, and you know it. And what's more to the point,' she stirred her coffee vigorously, even though she used neither sugar nor cream, 'why force me to resume that farce? Neither of us wants it.'

'So you do agree to come back to me?' He shifted slightly in his seat, leaning forward across the table and searching her stony features with eyes that didn't miss a trick.

'You've got me over a barrel.' Fliss hunched one shoulder, her face set and furious, and he grinned suddenly, wolfishly, making her shake.

'Hardly the most flattering of responses, but no matter.' He turned, beckoning for the bill. 'I have to be on the road by six in the morning, so I'll run you home now.' He scrawled his bold, decisive signature on the slip of paper, recapped his pen and slid it into an inner pocket. 'Just one more thing...' A cynical smile deepened the grooves at the sides of his mouth, but the steely eyes were cold. 'You walked out on me after eight weeks of marriage, no reason given—no valid reason—and now you're about to walk back into it. Granted, I needed to use pressure, but did you decide to resume your wifely duties for Gerald's sake, or for "Auld Lang Syne"?'

'You've got to be joking!' Sudden rage overwhelmed her. Having forced her to agree to return to him, he was acting in character—offloading her, packing her off home without even the most facile attempt to explain the reasons behind his desire to have her live as his wife again. Not even a spurious regret for the past, or the hope that second time around might be better. And he was calmly suggesting that she might have agreed to his ultimatum because she was secretly yearning to take up where they'd left off! Did he think she was mad—an unhinged masochist?

'Then it has to be for Gerald's sake. I was quite right.' He was on his feet now, waiting for her, jingling his car keys impatiently. He couldn't wait to be rid of her, and he still hadn't explained his reasons for using her this time round—for that was what he was doing.

'You and Gerald Harlie are very close; you have been for years. You even had breakfast with him this morning. You must have found my presence at dinner last night most inhibiting. Frustrating enough after a month's absence to send you over there as soon as you'd tumbled out of bed?'

'You put your spies on me!' she fizzed, hating him, hating the feeling that hired eyes were on her continually—at his behest. 'You're disgusting!'

They were outside now, their feet crunching on the gravel as they walked towards where his car was parked at the rear of the hotel. And she heard his low laughter in the moon-silvered darkness and shuddered, hurrying on; then the heel of one of her high, strappy sandals twisted beneath her, throwing her off balance.

Briefly, she swayed towards him and he caught her, steadying her against the length of his superb, hard body for a splintered fragment of time. Shatteringly, a sheet of molten sensation flooded her swaying body at the contact with his, and shock weakened her legs. But her instinct to yield to the support of his strength was only momentary, quickly ousted by common sense.

She pulled herself shakily out of the circle of his arms, her senses still stinging in the most humiliating way as she caught his bland words.

'What's disgusting about wanting to know what one's wife is doing—and with whom she is doing it?'

Unlocking the car door, he held it open for her, and she would have given much to be able to flounce away, cut him right out of her life as she had done before. But there was no way she could do that—not unless she was willing to see five hundred people thrown out of work—and she was too caught up with her own feeble impotency to do more than stare at him blankly when he added, 'What did Netta think about your relationship with her husband?'

Sapphire eyes shot him a glinting upwards glance as she slid reluctantly into her seat. Ruthless confidence was stamped on his features; it was part of his nature, born in him, bolstered by his snobbish family, and nothing was going to change it now. The first time she'd seen that look had been when he'd asked her to marry him, but then she'd been knocked sideways, rendered reeling and witless by the thought that the charming Leon Draker, the darling of ambitious society mamas and the focus of the secret fantasies of their nubile daughters, should actually be so arrogantly determined to marry a timid nobody like herself. The knowledge had been frightening and heady. And she had been so in love with him, too besotted to question his motives.

But Fliss knew better now, she knew exactly why he had chosen her. At twenty-two she was nobody's fool, and if he wanted to read something into her relationship with Gerald, then let him!

Savagely, she slammed the car door shut and waited, fuming, while he walked round and slid in beside her.

'Cat got your tongue? Or don't you like to think of your relationship with your boss as being common knowledge?' The harsh line of his profile was ungiving, and in the muted light from the dashboard she saw a muscle jerk at the side of his mouth. In any other man she would have put his obvious anger down to jealousy, but the idea of Leon Draker being jealous of her relationship with Gerald was too absurd even to think about.

Her soft, full lips set in an uncompromising line. He could think what he liked. Everyone who mattered knew that she and Gerald—not to mention Netta when she had been alive—had enjoyed a close, almost parent and child relationship. Leon Draker had a twisted mind.

'I'm surprised you didn't move in with him,' he said nastily, as if stung beyond endurance by her sulky silence.

She replied tartly, 'It was suggested, don't think it wasn't!' And not for anything would she give him the satisfaction of knowing that it had been Netta, dear Netta, who had suggested it several times because she had worried about the girl who had taken the place of the daughter she had never had. And, flicking him a sideways glance, she saw his mouth tighten, giving his profile a look of ferocity that made her shudder, despite the small triumph of needling him.

They had reached her street, and he drew up outside her door, keeping the engine gently ticking over. So he wasn't going to force his way in tonight, she thought, grateful for small mercies.

'I'll be back on Saturday,' he told her, his finger-tips drumming silently against the steering-wheel. 'That gives you four days to pack, and hand in your notice.'

The words were absorbed with difficulty by her stunned brain, and then she howled, 'I'm not leaving Harlie's!' The words were dragged out on a wail of disbelief. 'You can't make me give up my job—it's archaic!' she added, with a great deal more confidence than she felt.

'No? If you don't resign, I'll fire you.' His face was unreadable as he twisted round, lounging back in the angle of the door and window, his eyes enigmatic in the austerity of his shadowed face. 'The lawyers will have finished picking their way through the fine print by next week. The deal can go through as soon as I'm satisfied you've kept your side of the bargain.'

'I can't just walk out on Gerald.' She stared ahead, down the dark, empty street, trying to sound as though she were making a statement of fact. But she was on shaky ground, and she knew it. As soon as the merger went through he would have effective control; he could hire and fire at will.

Her blood ran cold. The only thing that had made her acceptance of his hateful ultimatum remotely tolerable had been the thought of her job at Harlie's and her tranquil flat. Leon Draker wouldn't show his face in Marton Clee more than absolutely necessary. He wasn't a small-town man. Thus, she had blithely reasoned, their resumed marriage need only be a weekend thing. And now he was taking even that consolation from her.

'What could I tell Gerald?' she persisted, resisting the impulse to tie her fingers into knots. 'I can't walk out like that.'

'You managed it four years ago,' he commented unanswerably. 'The job's no problem. I'll be bringing new people in—sales manager, finance controller, and so on. Tim Ormond will be out. He's merely a passenger, too. As far as I can make out, Harlie gave him a job as a favour to his father—as he gave you your job for favours of an entirely different kind.'

This was too much, too galling for words! Every muscle in her body tightened until she felt she was about to explode. After years of single-minded hard work he was stripping her of everything—independence, self-respect, self-confidence, everything! His opinion that Gerald had promoted her to sales manager because of her ability in bed made her feel terminally ill!

She was tempted to tell him that, far from resuming their marriage, she wanted a divorce—as soon as possible—and she shot upright in her seat, the angry words almost scalding her tongue when she swallowed them with an anguished groan and subsided heavily against the leather upholstery.

He hadn't been making idle threats when he'd said he would call the merger off unless she did precisely as he wanted. And despite her earlier, rather desperate optimism, she now knew that Harlie's needed this merger if they were to survive.

'Harlie's, as it is, doesn't stand a chance.' Leon unknowingly echoed her despairing thoughts. 'Gerald's no go-getter, and just lately he's lost control. As for the rest of the board, they're still rooted in the nineteenth century. If you want a job, try being a proper wife on for size. There's no way I'm leaving you here to be with sugar-daddy. You'll go where I can keep an eye on you, and as for Gerald—just tell him the truth. Tell him we've decided on a reconciliation.'

'Damn you!' Her hatred of him made her body tense, made the blood slam through her veins, and her movements were jerky as she got out of the car. He had an answer to everything, but it wasn't going to be easy to tell Gerald the truth—and not for the reasons Leon imagined!

Gradually, over the months of their getting to know each other, she had confided in Gerald and Netta. They had heard the bare outlines of her loveless, lonely childhood, and they had understood the basic insecurity that had come out of those early years. And they had helped her to understand that the fault had not been hers, that her parents hadn't been indifferent to her because she was unlovable.

But, although she had confided in them, she had never been able to bring herself to tell them about her marriage. She had always felt ashamed of that younger, gullible self. Telling Gerald now, after all this time, would hurt him, make him believe she had never trusted him and Netta enough to tell them the whole truth.

'Be ready to leave on Saturday.' Leon had wound down the window, and his voice came clearly on the still night air. Fliss froze, her shoulders rigid, her key held tightly between her fingers as he followed that remark with, 'And don't think you can walk out on me again as soon as the merger's gone through. I'll see you in hell before you do that to me again.'

## CHAPTER FOUR

'I DON'T believe this!' Gerald's heavy jawline sagged. 'You have been married to Leon Draker for four years?'

Fliss nodded, tension tying her in knots. It had been a hell of a week. Gerald had been summoned to the Draker building in the capital on Tuesday, ostensibly to liaise with the lawyers. But Fliss knew Leon had been behind it, had snapped his fingers and whisked the older man out of her orbit. And so she had had no opportunity to get together with her supposed lover. Hell, what a farce! Fliss set her teeth, her eyes ominously dark—Leon was a skunk to even think that she and Gerald were lovers!

He had returned this morning, Friday, and his first words to Fliss had been, 'You should have seen that building—big as a palace—and the penthouse suite—fantastic! It made my four-star hotel look like a doss-house!'

And Fliss had had to cut into his enthusiasm, his relief that the details for the proposed merger had been ironed out to everyone's satisfaction.

He had taken the news of her resignation hard, the news of her status as Leon's wife even harder. He felt, as she had known he must, hurt, not trusted.

'You didn't say a word—not even when he came to dinner that night,' he accused, his eyebrows lowering. And Fliss smoothed the olive-green fabric of her skirt over her knees and watched her fingers shake.

'It was over, had been for years. It was a terrible shock, meeting him again like that. I didn't think it would have helped to scream, or swoon!'

'No,' he commented drily. 'You simply snapped his head off.'

Fliss grimaced. If she had been able to bring herself to tell him the truth on the following morning, he wouldn't be feeling so hurt now. And they might have worked something out together if she'd told him of Leon's degrading ultimatum.

Unconsciously, she shook her head, repudiating that idea, her glossy dark hair glinting in the sunlight that slid in through the office windows. She could never have put that burden on Gerald's shoulders—asked him to choose between her personal happiness and the future of his company.

Tears stung her eyes; there would have been no competition. Gerald would have done what he had to do—persuaded her that the merger had to go ahead at all costs—and then spent the rest of his life feeling like a louse. She could never have done that to him.

Seeing the glitter of uncharacteristic tears, Gerald shifted uncomfortably in his chair. 'I'm sorry I barked, Fliss. It came as a shock. I just want you to know that I hope it works out for you both this time round.'

'And I'm sorry I had to spring it on you, that I'm leaving you in the lurch like this.' Fliss lifted troubled eyes to him, but he brushed her apology aside.

'Don't worry about a thing, but——' he shook his head, his eyes pained '—I don't think I'll ever get used to it. Leon Draker, your husband!' He ran his fingers through his thick, greying hair. 'How did you meet him? You must have married when you were barely out of school.'

'Almost,' she agreed wearily. She could tell him of the way they'd met, of their brief, mind-spinning courtship. But not the reason for the breakup—never that.

'My father and his family had recently left for America. I was just eighteen, and almost finishing my first year at college, rooming with another girl. Maire was a fledgling model, had good family connections, but felt stifled by them. She was full of life, brimming with self-confidence—we made strange flatmates!' Her mouth tilted wryly as she remembered the timid, over-serious, emotionally insecure girl she had been. 'Anyway, Maire had an invitation—she called it a Royal Command—to attend a cousin's engagement party at some glitzy London hotel, and she asked me to go along for moral support. She hadn't wanted to take her current manfriend because he was rabid left wing, and would have turned up in jeans and trainers and made rude comments about all the inevitable pearls and diamonds and dowagers. So I went, and that's where I met Leon. And I felt like, and was, such a mouse in those days, so I couldn't believe it when he drove me home and asked for a date. It was all quite unbelievable.'

She twisted her fingers together, feeling a dew of perspiration break out on her forehead. The memories were strong, even now. Memories of what it had felt like to be so ardently and openly pursued by a man such as Leon Draker: wealthy, sophisticated, so damnably sure of himself.

She had fallen in love so easily, so completely, and she had closed her ears to the cool voice of reason that had warned her that Leon was way out of her league, that the prince didn't marry the goose-girl—except in fairy-tales. And so she had accepted his proposal, afraid almost to breathe in case the spell was broken and she would wake up and find herself lonely, unwanted and unloved, with just the memory of a romantic, glittering dream to sustain her.

'Yes, unbelievable,' Gerald said heavily. 'Not because he wanted you, I don't mean that. You're an extremely beautiful young woman, and Netta and I often wondered why you never showed any interest in men.' He spread his square hands in a gesture of helplessness. 'But I find it hard to believe you never confided in Netta. She loved you, Fliss—as if you were her own. She would have been terribly hurt if she'd discovered you didn't trust her enough to tell her something like that.'

It was all there—in his eyes, in the weary slump of his shoulders. He felt betrayed. And Fliss, her generous heart hurting with contrition, with the need to reassure because she knew exactly what betrayal felt like, got quickly to her feet, her vivid blue eyes compassionate.

'Gerald——' She was on his side of the desk, one hand on his dejected shoulder. 'I've always trusted you and Netta more than anyone else I've ever known. I have good reason to. You both cared about me, helped me to know myself in a way I might possibly never have worked out for myself. How could I not have trusted you—both of you!'

His hand came up to cover hers and she met his eyes, saw the depth of paternal affection there, and smiled shakily.

'I couldn't talk about my marriage, not even to myself. I'd shut it and Leon right out of my head. Believe me?'

'Of course.' His fingers tightened over hers. 'And I know everything will work out for you this time. Your husband's a great guy, one of the best.'

'Thank you.' Her eyes were glazed with tears. Gerald really cared about her, and she couldn't tell him that her life with Leon, this time round, would be as disastrous as it had been before. Briefly, she dropped a light kiss on his cheek, and a voice from the doorway slid in between them, like a cobra.

'I've come to collect my wife, Harlie. I take it the sorrowful farewells are over and she's free to go?'

'Ah, Draker.' If Gerald noticed the grim look of fury on the hard man's face, he certainly didn't let it trouble him. He pushed himself to his feet, and after a brief, intense look in Fliss's direction, faced Leon, his smile urbane. 'Fliss has just been telling me that you and she have been married for years.'

'Yes, I guessed that much.' Leon's smoky eyes held the older man's, and the look of compassion in the steady gaze surprised Fliss, who would have sworn her husband incapable of feeling any such thing for anyone. 'It must have come as a shock.'

The truth in that statement made Gerald's mouth tighten, though not for the reason Leon obviously had in mind as he placed a proprietorial arm around Fliss's shoulders, hard determination replacing the formal veiling of pity.

'Ready to go, darling?'

She could only shrug at that; there was nothing to be gained by drawing attention to the way she really felt. It would upset Gerald too much if he guessed the truth.

'Almost. I have one or two things to collect from my office. So I'll say *au revoir*, Gerald.' Her eyes were soft as she held out a slim hand and felt her boss's fingers tighten affectionately over her own. 'Keep in touch.'

'I'll do that—you just try to stop me! And, Fliss, be happy.'

She had to get out of the room quickly, before her expression betrayed her. Apart from Netta, Gerald was the best friend she had ever had, and Leon was forcing them apart, tearing her away from the job she had worked so hard to deserve, and no way would she ever be happy with the man who had once taken her loving heart and trampled it beneath his feet!

Brushing past Leon with barely a glance at his stony, closed features, she almost ran to her office, where she emptied her desk-drawers of the accumulation of personal bits and pieces, thrusting them haphazardly into a plastic carrier she'd brought for the purpose. He had followed her, she noted with irritation, and was leaning against the door-frame, grim-faced and silent. To stop herself worrying over the implications of what she was doing, she snapped, 'You told me to be ready to leave on Saturday. Today, if you recall, is Friday!'

'So it is.' He didn't move, he was totally still—except for his eyes, and they followed her every movement. 'I decided to fetch you today. Let's put it down to an understandable eagerness to resume our married life.' He smiled suddenly, the lines on either side of his mouth deepening sardonically, and she stuffed an unopened pack of tights into the carrier and flashed him a look of intense dislike. He was no more eager than she to re-embark on the farce of their marriage—he had no hair-shirt inclinations, as far as she knew.

But for some devious reason of his own he needed a wife at the moment, even if only a paper one, and, having blackmailed her into accepting the position, he was, quite characteristically, ordering her around with no regard for her own needs or wishes.

'We'll leave as soon as we've picked up your gear,' he stated, underlining her rebellious thoughts, and she turned on him, her hands on her generous hips, her eyes glittering.

'And if I'm not ready to leave?' Her breath was coming quickly, making her full breasts rise and fall rapidly, pushing against the thin fabric of her blouse and commanding the attention of his knowing eyes. His slow, assessing look made her pulses race—it was as though he were fondling her physically, and she recognised her body's shaming reaction, felt her breasts harden and peak.

Disgust with herself for allowing him to affect her that way refuelled her anger, and she bit out, 'Just because I was forced to agree to your hateful ultimatum, it doesn't mean I'm willing to be treated like a mindless idiot!'

'Felicity——' A long sigh escaped him as he levered his long body away from the door-frame. 'Quit fighting me, can't you? I take it you are packed?' And, without waiting for a reply to that, 'There's no point at all in our hanging around here. We may as well make tracks.'

He was right, damn him! She was finished in Marton Clee—no job and, as from tomorrow morning, no home. There was little point in dragging the agony of departure out for longer than need be. But she wasn't about to admit that to him, and she gathered her things together and walked out of her office for the last time, tight-lipped, without a backward glance.

The short journey to her flat was accomplished in taut silence. Apart from packing the clothes she had intended to wear tomorrow, there was little to do. She had already sold her old Mini to a youngster on the shop floor, and now she just had to lock the door behind her and hand the key to Miss Pargeter, who had promised to let in the removal men who would be arriving on Monday to take the personal odds and ends she'd put into packing cases into store.

Leon had already taken her two large suitcases down to the car, and Fliss was packing the unused food-stuffs from the store cupboards and fridge into a carton. She would give them to Miss P, along with the key, and she was concentrating on that, not giving herself time to look around, because if she took a long look at the loved home she was being forced to abandon she would burst into messy, childish tears.

'Almost finished?' Leon had walked into the room and was looking out of the single, tiny window which afforded a view of the dustbins in the yard and the single lilac bush which valiantly bloomed each spring, its spicy perfume filling the small area.

She looked at him and she hated him. He was dragging her, mentally kicking and screaming, away from the life she had made for herself, and there was nothing she could do about it. She had never felt so impotent.

'Where are we going?' She had a right to know. 'And don't say ''Feathergay'' because I refuse to set foot inside that house ever again.' She had spent the unhappiest eight weeks of her life there. She would always associate it with heartbreak and humiliation, with the death of her marriage. It seemed so strange that so lovely a place could be so hateful.

He turned his head and looked at her coldly. 'No one's asking you to; it would be the last thing Annabel could stomach.'

Fliss digested this in silence. His statement came as no shock to her. Annabel Draker had always hated her; she made a fit mother for this man.

She made a small, throwaway gesture with one pretty hand. 'Where are we going, then?'

'To the penthouse for the time being.' He took the unopened bottle of milk she was holding and added it to the contents of the carton. 'Later, of course, you will have to visit Feathergay. After all, you will be mistress there one day.'

And wouldn't Annabel loathe the idea of that! she thought with bitter humour. Her mother-in-law loved that house as though it were a living thing, and her devotion had infected her only son. There had been Drakers at Feathergay since the Restoration, when it had been built, and Annabel had made it crystal-clear that she didn't think Fliss fit to cross the threshold.

She pushed the carton of groceries at him, and cast a last brief look around the room, then ground out, through constricting throat muscles, 'I have no interest in Feathergay now, and don't intend taking any in the future. If it burned to the ground in the night, I wouldn't blink an eyelash.'

He might have forced her to return to him, but he wasn't going to have things all his own way. He would soon discover just how much she had changed.

'If you want a mistress for your family home,' she advised coldly, 'your best course would be to divorce me and marry someone who would be willing to sacrifice her identity to an impeccable pedigree and a pile of stones and mortar.'

The light went out of his eyes. 'There will be no divorce, you can be sure of that.' The bones of his face hardened beneath taut skin, and he turned away quickly. 'Shall we go?' he said, and if she hadn't known better she would have said he looked like a man who had just received a devastating blow. But that was nonsense, because he must know how much she disliked Feathergay and its unhappy associations.

Tired of the seemingly interminable journey, of Leon's silence, of her own bleak thoughts, Fliss asked, a barb in her voice, 'Does Annabel know we're getting back together? I don't suppose she's exactly over the moon about it.' Then she watched from the corner of her eye and saw the unexpected twitch of a muscle at the side of his mouth. But his voice was dead-pan, not telling her whether the quirk of his mouth denoted ire or amusement.

'She knows.'

'And she's out right now, killing the fatted calf?' Fliss hazarded sardonically. 'She always hated me.'

'Not always,' he contradicted evenly. 'Not until the day you walked out on me and left her to break the news that you were sick of the sight of me, that I was on no account to try to reach you. That you were going back to a former boyfriend—someone of your own age.'

So Annabel had told him that, had she? Fliss could believe it. True, she had spoken to her mother-in-law on that dreadful day, asked her to convey a message to Leon. But not that message.

As far as Fliss had known, Leon had still been in bed with Edwina, oblivious to the rest of the world—certainly to the fact that his wife had walked into that room and into a nightmare. She had seen Leon's dark head on the pillow, heard him murmur something, but after that her shocked eyes had been riveted on Edwina . . . Edwina turning lazily from Leon, rising up against the pillows, her naked body as mocking as her glinting green eyes and her curving mouth. She had laughed, low in her throat, a triumphant ripple of sound that had made Fliss's heart freeze, and she had known that everything Edwina and Annabel had ever said was absolutely, undeniably true.

Hardly able to think straight at the time, Fliss had gathered a few of her possessions together, stuffing them haphazardly into a grip, and had been already half-way down Feathergay's impressive driveway on her way to the village bus-stop when she'd met her mother-in-law on her way back from walking the dogs.

Fliss could still see the contemptuous look in the older woman's eyes as she'd queried, 'In a hurry, are we?'. She could still feel the sharpness of the autumnal afternoon air, smell the tanginess of rotting leaves, of bonfire smoke and misty air.

'Yes. Would you give Leon a message for me? Tell him I'm leaving. Our marriage is over.' She had meant to write as soon as she'd found somewhere to hide herself—even then she hadn't wanted him to worry over her whereabouts—as if he would! But Annabel would doubtless be happy to save her that chore. 'Tell him not to bother to try to find me, and tell him——' her precarious control had teetered then '—tell him he can divorce me and marry Edwina. It's what they both want.'

But that had been a long time ago, and the pain had been translated to anger, an anger so intense that it made her want to throw back her head and howl for the innocent, trusting, feeble fool she had been four years ago. Instead, she pushed bitter memories back into limbo, where they belonged, and fixed her dry, burning eyes on the monotonous motorway ahead.

'And you believed her, of course.'

'Why shouldn't I? She would hardly make something like that up.' He sounded very cool, very laid-back, as if it had all happened to someone on another planet. He didn't know that Fliss had seen him in bed with Edwina—unless that aristocratic little lady had deemed it politic to tell him—and the news of his unwanted wife's departure would have given him nothing but relief. 'After a week of wedded bliss,' his mouth curved acidly, 'I knew our marriage had been a mistake. Every time I looked at you, you flinched. Every time you looked at me you resembled a kicked spaniel. And as for our lovemaking—that was non-existent. You were nothing but a doll. Empty. When I tried to make love to you, you froze. It made sense that you'd gone, gone to someone else. Someone younger. It was the truth, after all, wasn't it? Annabel doesn't lie, so why shouldn't I have believed her?'

'No reason,' Fliss countered bitterly. Annabel had been careful to mask her intense disapproval of the young and unsuitable daughter-in-law her son had presented her with. She had kept her insults, her cruelly denigrating remarks, for such times as Leon was absent. And he would have preferred to believe those lies because they left him free to be with the woman he really wanted. His conscience, if he had one, would have rested more easily.

She stared moodily out of the window, not bothering to contradict him, to tell him exactly why Annabel should have lied four years ago. Because it really didn't matter. Nothing would alter the fact that he had married her for revenge, that he had immediately regretted it and had been glad to be rid of her. Nothing would alter the fact that his love for Edwina had been strong enough to shatter his marriage vows.

And during the short time with him at Feathergay, as his wife, she had been humiliated enough to last her a lifetime. She was not going to court further humiliation by letting him know, now, that she had left him because her heart had been breaking up. Better, far better for her pride's sake, for him to believe his mother's lies.

'Well, at least you did as I asked and didn't try to find me,' she reflected drily, picking out the only part of the message Annabel had relayed truthfully.

He moved his eyes from the road for just long enough to flick her a frigid glance. 'I had you traced immediately, and have kept tabs on you ever since. I have always known where you were living, where you were working. If you'd hoped I'd come after you, begging, just to give you an ego-trip, you didn't know me very well. I don't beg, Felicity. Remember that.'

He reached forward and slipped a tape into the deck, and above the strangely haunting music of Enya he told her slowly, 'Shortly after you left, my father died. After that I had my hands full with Annabel, with the business. Father had been ill for some time, but none of us had suspected a thing. To put it politely, his affairs were in a mess. I spent years, literally, chasing myself all over the world, until I sometimes thought I'd meet myself coming back. And if you think that's a crazy statement, that's what that period in my life was like. Crazy. I worked myself to a standstill, pulling the business back together again, making it stronger, invulnerable. I certainly didn't have time to chase after a wife who'd admitted she couldn't stand the sight of me.'

'I'm sorry,' Fliss said quietly. She meant for the death of his father. Nigel Draker had been an unknown quantity to her. They had met on one occasion only, at her wedding, and he had seemed to like her, to genuinely welcome her to the family. Recently returned from an extended European business trip, he had taken off almost immediately after the reception to finalise some merger or other in Hong Kong. He had still been away when she had left Leon.

'Don't be,' he advised heavily. 'The past is done with. Our future's the only thing that should concern you now.' And with that ominous remark he lapsed into silence, leaving Fliss to brood over far from relaxing thoughts.

A private lift from the car park beneath the Draker building transported them to the penthouse suite. Fliss deliberately wasted time as she stepped from the discreet metal box into the lounge, giving the spacious room her closest inspection. She felt shaky now, suddenly confused, definitely not up to being alone with Leon, on his home ground.

The room was luxurious, though basically functional, decorated in shades of grey which ranged from the pearly white of the carpets and walls, through soft dove shades for curtains and upholstery, to the deep charcoal of the leather couches. And it was quiet—very quiet. Down below, the city streets throbbed and growled, but the traffic noises didn't impinge at this rarefied height.

'Nice.' She thought some comment was due, if only to break the electric silence, and she made it drily and was rewarded by a glinting little smile.

'I'm glad you approve, since this will be our main base for the time being. I wouldn't want you to feel uncomfortable.'

As if he cared a rap for her comfort, she thought acidly. She was here for a purpose, and sooner or later she would discover what it was.

'Are we alone?' All at once the thought horrified her, and he nodded.

'Yes, I gave Spike the evening off. Does it bother you?' At her deliberately blank stare, which she hoped would hide the fact that, for some reason, she was bothered a great deal, he added, 'He will have left us a cold supper—unless you would prefer to eat out.'

She shrugged, showing a lack of interest. She would have preferred not to eat at all—at least, not with him—but didn't say so. The atmosphere was suddenly, frighteningly electric, and the tingle of fear which had prickled over her skin as soon as she had stepped inside his home was growing more intense by the moment. But she would die before giving him an inkling of that weakness. If she displayed any weakness whatsoever, he would seize on it, use it to his own advantage.

'Who's Spike, when he's at home,' she asked, taking care to make her question casual.

'Alfred Manley Spiker, to give him his full name. Ex-pugilist. He's been looking after me for three years.'

'I see.' Fliss made a show of studying one of the several water-colours that hung on the walls, although she took nothing in except a vague blur of colour. She had no idea why she should suddenly feel so tense, so afraid. She could almost see herself shaking. 'A male housekeeper—how interesting. Or is he more of a bodyguard? Have you made enough enemies to feel you need one?'

Her bravado must have worked, hiding her fear, because his only reaction to her gibe was a slight sideways smile as he picked up her suitcases.

'I'll show you to your bedroom, as Spike's not around to do the honours. And I'd better warn you, he's very dignified, and will expect you to be the same. He rules the apartment absolutely. He has rules and very little patience.'

A dignified ex-boxer? Fliss might have found that amusing if her heart hadn't been pounding fit to choke her as she followed him into a wide, lushly carpeted inner hallway.

He had paused at one of the many doors, pushing it open with a shrug of one wide shoulder, and she found enough composure from somewhere to toss a languid question, which was really not a question at all.

'I hope your minder has given me a room of my own? I have no intention of sleeping with you.'

There was a silence, very brief, but very taut, filled with things unsaid, with the tension that had been mounting since she had entered the penthouse, until he broke it, a tauntingly wicked glimmer in his eyes.

'Who said I wanted you to?' He pushed the door wider, and revealed a perfectly appointed yet impersonal room, gesturing towards the narrow single bed. 'I have other uses for you, Felicity. I wonder if they'll be as abhorrent to you as the idea of sharing my bed has always been.'

## CHAPTER FIVE

For fully three minutes she stood in the centre of the deep-piled fern-green carpet, staring at the cocooning soft russet walls. Her emotions were in a state of upheaval, the sort of derangement she had successfully schooled out of her life—until his re-emergence on the scene.

Upon entering the penthouse she had felt afraid, and hadn't known the reason for it until relief at the sight of the single bed had made that reason clear. She had been terrified that he would insist she share his bed as well as his roof and his name. The merger hadn't been finalised yet, and that would have been one more stick to beat her into submission.

So why the insidious clenching pain, deep inside her? Why the agony in her breast where once her heart had been? It didn't make the remotest sense. He had stated unequivocally that he had no desire to take her to his bed, and that was definitely the way she wanted it. So why the pain?

Disgusted with herself, she wiped the clammy palms of her hands down the sides of her skirt, making a small *moue* of distaste. And as for that enigmatic rider concerning the unspecified 'other uses' he had for her—well, she would just have to find out what those uses were and block them.

She was in a situation not of her choosing, but she had to make the best of it and show him she was not a puppet to be manipulated to suit his whims. And, for a start, if this was to be her room, then there must be changes.

She cast a dispassionate eye over her surroundings: simple, luxurious—a carpet that swallowed the feet, ample built-in wardrobe and drawer space—but soulless. Something would have to be done...

'Would you like a cup of tea?' The innocuous remark, coming from the doorway, shattered her carefully guarded composure, and she flinched visibly, her eyes growing enormous in their sockets.

'No. No, thanks.' Her lips felt thick, almost unmanageable, and she clamped them together, feeling the tremor of warm flesh against her teeth. He had shed his suit jacket, and his white lawn shirt was open at the neck, his tie carelessly askew. He looked relaxed and dangerous, his mouth softening in a smile that took her breath away because it transported her back four years. That old devastating charm was there, the charm that had left her defenceless, a pliable slave.

But the casual lift of one strongly defined eyebrow told a more up-to-date story. It told of the mocking, arrogant will that he so successfully cloaked with that silken, deadly charm.

'Not settled in yet, darling?' Lazy grey eyes flicked to the unpacked cases. 'Not to worry, we'll eat at seven. Spike has left us amply provisioned. You don't want to go out, do you?' He was talking as if she had choices, but he was making all the decisions, and she could have hit him for that alone. Instead, she turned to the window, pulling aside the fern-green curtains, looking out blindly, seeing nothing, willing him to go.

'Not feeling talkative?' There was a hint of laughter hidden beneath the velvety tones, and her stomach muscles clenched, her hands bunching into tight little fists at her sides. He was tormenting her, damn him! He had the upper hand, and he knew it, and revelled in it. He was loathsome!

'Tired, darling?' His voice crossed the room like a caress, and she shuddered, her back rigidly turned on him. 'Why don't you have a shower, relax? Sleep for a while on your narrow little bed? You'll be quite safe.' The soft voice hardened. 'I won't join you there until you beg me to.'

And that would never be! Fliss vowed, hearing the click of the door-latch as he left the room. Fighting back choking, idiotic tears, she turned from the window. The trouble was, there had been a time when she had been desperate for his lovemaking. Too desperate, perhaps. She had loved him and longed for him, been impatient for the passionate kisses—the caresses he had taken so far and no further—to be extended, to deepen and widen, to encompass them both until they were fulfilled in the final act of love, an act which would bond them for all time.

But her basic insecurity, born in childhood and reinforced by Annabel's hostile reception, had made her feel somehow unworthy, unfit for the love of her older, sophisticated husband. She had been so afraid she would fail him on their wedding night—her fear so great that she had ended up doing just that. Fear of failure had created it.

She hadn't been able to explain it to him, and only partially to herself, but he had held her trembling body in his arms that night, had wiped her tears away with a gentle hand before turning away from her, saying that everything would be all right, given time. But it hadn't been all right. It had grown worse. Fliss's small amount of self-confidence had been dissipated utterly by her own failure, by Annabel's private and cold disparagement. How could a gauche, eighteen-year-old virgin who, up until then, had never inspired love in another human being, hope to satisfy the urbane twenty-nine-year-old worldly-wise man who was her husband?

The type of woman who would hold his interest, satisfy his mental and physical needs for longer than it took to make love to her, would be someone perfectly presented, witty and sparkling.

So why had he married her? the younger Fliss had agonised. She was barely out of school, with no visible accomplishments—plump, shy, badly dressed—she was, as Annabel had implied, pretty much a disaster. And so she had worried, heartbroken and ashamed because Leon had taken another bedroom after only one week of married life, appalled because he was more often away from home than not, leaving her to try to cope with his mother's scathing comments.

And then his second cousin, the cynical, beautiful Edwina, had told her exactly why Leon Draker, heir to a huge business empire and one of the finest small manor houses in the country, had married the first unsuitable but willing female he had laid his eyes on.

But her information had come too late, because by the time Edwina's ice-green eyes had swept over her in narrowed contempt as she had coolly imparted those reasons, it had been much too late. She had been married to Leon for exactly five weeks.

He had married her for the harshest of reasons: revenge. Even as Edwina had spoken, everything clicked into place, the unbelievable becoming shamingly credible. How often, during their whirlwind courtship, had she asked herself, 'Why me?', unable to understand why a man such as Leon Draker should have fallen in love with her, wanted her for his wife. She had no elevated background, none of the qualities to attract and hold a man who was wealthy, sophisticated, able to have his pick of the many available women of his own class—beautiful, slender, sparkling women—women like Edwina.

'I'm sorry for you,' Edwina had said, her glittering eyes holding something very remote from pity. 'You're the one who's going to be hurt by all this—not Leon, not me. He's a ruthless swine, but you weren't to know that, were you? Look, can I get you a drink? You look as if you need one.'

'No.' Shock had made her curt. The too rapid beat of her heart had been suffocating her. She had known that what she was about to hear was going to be unbearable, the realisation of her worst fears, the fears that had plagued her since she had come to this beautiful, ancient house as Leon's unsuitable bride.

'Leon and I have always known we'd marry eventually.' The skirts of Edwina's elegant dress had whispered as she'd moved across the quiet, panelled study to the drinks cupboard. She had been very self-assured, her slender body and impeccable grooming making Fliss feel like a bundle of old washing. 'We've known each other forever, of course, though up until about ten years ago we did nothing but fight.'

Edwina had been standing in the mullioned stone window embrasure then, a fluted glass in her hands.

'I was sixteen when it happened. When we stopped sparring and became lovers. Nothing could be done about it then, naturally.' The tinkling laugh had knifed Fliss's heart. She wanted to get up and leave the room, but she was incapable of movement. So she sat, staring at the floor, wretched and miserable, dreading what was to come.

'Leon was twenty, still at university, and I had two more years at my boarding school and another two at a Swiss finishing school to get through. But we managed to meet quite often—oh, lord, we were wild for each other! It was like a fever. It still is. Oh, we've had our fights—it's inevitable when two people love as we do. We each played around, but nothing serious. Neither of us ever went too far with those others—we used to compare notes!'

She had laughed huskily, and Fliss had felt her cheeks burn with embarrassment and turned her head to hide her face as Edwina had told her, 'Then came the big one. Row, I mean. It blew up over something trivial—our families had decided we were to marry last December, and Leon had agreed—without consulting me first. I wanted a June wedding and I told him I wasn't going to be pushed around. After all,' she had paced gracefully over the Persian carpet, sinking down in a leather club chair, 'we both knew we were already bound inextricably together—so a few more months of single life wouldn't hurt each other. And I had a winter skiing holiday with an Austrian baron and his party tied up. I didn't want to miss that, which I would have done had we kowtowed to the parents and married in December. Anyway,' she had shrugged elegantly, 'Leon and I had a furious fight. He accused me of making a play for the baron, so—naturally—I did just that. And the whole thing went further than I'd intended. Much, much further. And Leon found out.'

She had drained her glass and set it down on a small side-table, and Fliss had flinched at the manufactured concern in the slow, cultured drawl.

'Predictably, he decided to pay me back. He told me he would. He was out of his mind with fury—and jealousy. And before anyone knew what the idiot was up to, he went out and married the first gullible little fool he could find.'

'I don't believe you,' Fliss had said thickly. But she *had* believed the other woman, believed every killing word. It had made horrible, logical sense.

That Leon possessed an anger so deep, a passion so intense, was something she had learned to recognise during these past five weeks. A deep and brooding passion lay behind his outward urbanity; it was something she had sensed on their wedding night. It had frightened her, because she hadn't known how to respond to it. And he, not loving her, had not had the patience to gentle her, to break through the barriers presented by a shy, insecure virgin of eighteen.

'Then you ought to believe me,' Edwina had advised coldly. 'The truth's often painful, but if you come to terms with it, it becomes bearable. Can you honestly say Leon's making you deliriously happy?' She lit a cigarette, blowing a thin plume of smoke into the air, her smile feline and frightening. 'And before you rush in to answer that with a loyal little lie, Annabel tells me that he's away more often than not, and that he's moved back into the bedroom he used as a boy. That doesn't sound like the action of a doting bridegroom.' She ground the half-finished cigarette out with a purposeful movement of jewelled fingers. 'I'm sorry, but nothing can kill the love Leon and I have for each other. Nothing!' Edwina had risen fluidly, her green eyes filled with scorn. 'We'll be lovers until he throws you out; I think you ought to know that. Right now, he still thinks he's punishing me, and I dare say I owe him that much. But sooner or later he'll get rid of you, and, after the inevitable divorce, he'll marry me. He won't be able to help himself.'

But Leon hadn't divorced her, and he hadn't married Edwina, Fliss thought broodingly. So something must have happened since that horrible interview four years ago. But Edwina had been correct in one of her forecasts: Leon had forgiven her, sooner, probably, than even Edwina had expected. Because three weeks later Fliss had walked into his room and found them in bed together.

She sighed drearily. There was no mileage in raking over the past. She knew why Leon had married her, but she didn't know why he had gone to the trouble to keep tabs on her, to secure a position from which he could blackmail her into agreeing to resume the marriage. It was something she was going to have to find out. She had a right to know.

Leadenly, she began to unpack her clothes. The very act was distasteful—it underlined the permanency of her position here, a position she hadn't sought and certainly didn't want.

But it need only last as long as it took to see the merger finalised, she reminded herself forcefully. No power on earth would keep her here once Harlie's was safe. In four years she had changed out of all recognition. She had come a long way in a relatively short space of time; she was polished, honed, hardened. Leon wouldn't find it so easy to intimidate her, push her around. It was something he would find himself learning once her obligation to Gerald, to the Harlie workforce, had been fulfilled.

Her wide, soft mouth was set in a line of grim determination as she closed a drawer on a pile of filmy undies, and she carried the now empty cases to a space in the huge built-in wardrobe. Turning from stowing them, her eyes were drawn to a set of bookshelves set in the space between the wardrobe and the bedroom door.

Idly, she ran her eyes over the titles. Romances, the latest offering from the pen of Ellis Peters, the complete works of Jane Austen, and a beautifully bound copy of Byron's poems. All were brand new, unread. Had he remembered her taste in reading matter and picked this selection out for her pleasure?

Hardly. She stripped off her suit, her underwear, and shrugged into a robe, taking the pins from her hair and shaking her head slowly from side to side so that its tumbled mass rioted around her shoulders. That the books had been provided specifically for her was in no doubt. But Leon had probably asked Spike to buy them. 'Get a dozen or so books,' he would have said. 'My wife enjoys reading.' It was, after all, just conceivable that he had remembered that much about her.

Dismissing the subject from her mind, she entered the en-suite bathroom. Very sumptuous, she noted, refusing to be impressed by the obvious expense that had gone into the furnishing of the entire penthouse suite. She had been tongue-tied, speechless and shaken with awe when she had first encountered the discreet opulence of Feathergay. She was not so easily impressed now.

Terracotta tiles carried over the colour scheme of the adjoining bedroom, and contrasted with pearly grey porcelain fitments, thick fern-green towels and bronze taps and towel-rails. A long smoked-glass shelf held lavish crystal jars of essences and body lotions, talcs and soaps, perfumes and toilet waters. All in the perfume that had always been her favourite.

She had treated herself to a small bottle of Joy as a confidence booster before she had gone to that fateful party with Maire. And after Leon had driven her home that night he had kissed her, very gently, but with a thoroughness that had shaken her, and he'd said, 'I love your perfume—you must always wear it. It might have been created for you.'

Her head spinning with a queer mixture of fright and stinging happiness, hardly able to believe that this amazingly charismatic man had insisted on driving her home—had even demanded to see her again—she had told him the name of the perfume, babbling because she hadn't known how to talk to him, how to cope with the feelings that, even then, were being born inside her. And he had merely smiled, a slow, haunting smile that had remained in her heart, warming her whenever she thought about it.

And now something came to life inside her, twisting and leaping in a parody of those long-forgotten feelings. Quickly, she dropped her robe on a stool and stepped beneath the shower. The idea that that unknown quantity, Alfred Manley Spiker, had purchased her precise choice in reading matter and the Joy toiletries was too much of a coincidence. Leon must have given specific instructions, or had actually set out to buy the things himself. She didn't know whether to be touched or terrified.

He had married her for the harshest of reasons, and yet, when they had first met, she had believed him to be the gentlest, kindest man alive. But surely he had not bought these things to please her? It was hardly possible that the sensitivity she had sensed in him all those years ago was still somewhere beneath the complex layers of his personality.

No. Unconsciously, Fliss shook her head in firm denial of that possibility. Four years ago she had been seeing what she had wanted to see. Edwina had opened her eyes to the truth, and no way was she going to go around wearing the blinkers of youthful inexperience again.

The books and toiletries had been given for a purpose, just as he had insisted on the resumption of their marriage for a specific purpose. He knew precisely what he was doing. But if he thought that by seeming to have her pleasure at heart he was softening her up, making her more willing to accept the restrictions he had placed upon her, then was he in for a surprise!

She dressed casually for dinner. No way was she aiming to give him the impression that this was in any way a special occasion. Her hair tightly pinned back, the amount of make-up she had used modest, she stared at her reflection in the full-length mirror, a pucker of dissatisfaction between her brows. The softly gathered, fine black cotton skirt worn with a silky white top did nothing at all to conceal her sensually curved body. Apart from making sure she was well-groomed, she rarely took notice of the way she looked, and was disinterested enough to be totally unaware of the way she affected members of the opposite sex. But now, for some reason, she was seeing herself with new eyes, completely aware of her own sexuality.

Frowning, she clipped an enamelled pendant on a fine gold chain around her neck, then hurriedly removed it. The colourful pendant drew attention to the valley between her full breasts, which the narrow V-neckline of the top she wore revealed.

About to rummage through her drawers for a concealing scarf, she heard the rap of fingers on the door.

'It's on the table; come and get it!' He sounded slightly impatient, as if he had expected her to join him long before now and was tired of waiting. But although she strained her ears listening for the comfortable sound of departing footsteps, none came. He was waiting for her, out there in the passage, and if she didn't go out at once he would come in and fetch her. She didn't want him in her room.

'I hope you're hungry.' He was lounging against the wall space opposite her door, and she felt the warm assessment of his eyes, then met the lingering, enigmatic look as he added ambiguously, 'I know I am.'

His fingers gripped her arm just above her elbow, and her flesh burned with sudden awareness as he walked her along the thickly carpeted passage. Suddenly, she was painfully conscious of him as a man, stingingly aware of the gracefully lean body clothed in narrow black cords, a black silk shirt opened at the neck to reveal the corded strength of his throat, the olive-toned skin of his chest.

Her breath clogged in her throat as she took herself in hand, firmly admonishing herself for allowing him to get to her on that level. On any level. The only way she could survive this period in her life was to remain impervious to anything he said or did.

Spike and his master had gone to a great deal of trouble, she thought, an ironic twist to her mouth as her eyes swept over the two low tables Leon had pulled up in front of one of the leather upholstered sofas. The polished surfaces were covered with every kind of cold food imaginable, and Fliss said, 'I couldn't eat a thing.'

She knew she was being dog-in-the-mangerish and she eyed the smoked salmon curls, salads, thin slices of beef and pheasant regretfully.

There was a hauntingly wicked glimmer in his eyes as he told her, 'Then I'll have to make inroads for both of us. That will be no problem at all, and I can't have Spike disappointed after all the trouble he's been to. You will have some wine, though?' One eyebrow was raised tauntingly, and she nodded, sinking down on one end of the squashy sofa, angling her back into the corner as she watched him walk over to a side-table.

That indolent grace had been one of the first things she had noticed about him, and it still had the power to move her, as anything beautiful always did.

But his physical presence was merely a cloak, hiding the real man. He was a man of many parts, all of them differing. There were so many elusive facets to his personality: the charm he could turn on at will, coaxing others to do whatever he wanted of them; the tough shrewdness that enabled him to control a huge and still growing business empire; the cruelty in him that had made him capable of marrying her in order to exact some kind of warped revenge on the woman he hungered for. He had inherited power and wealth and, from an early age, had been taught how to use it.

Reluctantly, she conceded that she had a tough fight ahead of her, and she accepted the flute of foaming, pale amber liquid he handed her and raised wary eyes.

'Champagne?'

'I thought the occasion called for a celebration.' He was beside her now, his nearness unsettling her, and she watched him cagily as he helped himself to the delicious food. 'You won't change your mind?' He offered her the plate and she shook her head stubbornly, hoping her stomach wouldn't rumble and give her away. He shrugged. 'You are being childish, Felicity. Why don't you stop fighting me and make the best of the situation, of our relationship? After all, you chose it, four years ago.'

His effrontery took her breath away, and her eyes sparked defiance, but she said nothing, summoning her resources.

'So shall we call a truce, try to live as civilised adults?' he questioned when he realised she had no comment to make. He turned, facing her, putting the plate of food back on the table, and he was sending out the signals she remembered too well—the slow, slightly off-centre smile, the lazily lowered eyelids which turned his irises to a slumbrous, smoky grey. Signals that had made the eighteen-year-old Felicity ready to drop at his feet.

But not any more—not if she could help it. Those invitingly sensual looks hadn't meant anything then, and they certainly didn't now. Her dry mouth, her hammering pulses, merely signified anger.

Her eyes froze as she met the lazy, inviting warmth in his, and her tone was frigid as she clipped, 'Four years ago I didn't know how many beans made five.

I was gormless enough to imagine our marriage could work. I know better now.'

'Do you?' His mouth tightened, the charming mask slipping to reveal a dark intentness. 'You didn't give our marriage a chance.' His face was austere, tight-fleshed, and there was a derisory dent at one side of his mouth. 'Or perhaps you realised that the material possessions I could offer in no way made up for the loss of your lover. Exciting, was he?'

Fliss went cold, but she kept hold of herself, managing a disinterested shrug. But she saw from the sudden glitter of his eyes just how much that seemingly careless gesture had annoyed him. Excellent, she told herself stoically. Better for her self-respect, her pride, for him to believe Annabel's lies. Though how he, of all men, could imagine that a woman, once in love with him, could willingly leave him for another man was beyond her comprehension.

'I think I'll go to bed now. I'm tired.' She rose fluidly, holding on to her self-control with an effort, unaware of the way her soft skirts swayed around her long, shapely legs, the fabric moulding itself to her hips and thighs. Just a few paces would bring her to the door, to blessed escape from his presence, but he was on his feet in one lithe movement, his hard fingers biting into the soft flesh of her arm.

'I haven't finished with you yet.'

'You're hurting me!' Her tone was cold as her eyes met his defiantly—glittering sapphire limned with thick charcoal lashes—and his own eyes narrowed, his fingers biting even deeper.

'The way I feel, I could do more than merely hurt you.' He jerked her closer to his lean, hard length, his eyes darkening as her breasts were forced into contact with the silk of his shirt.

Shamefully, Fliss felt her body's reaction to the contact, and her breath came rapidly, fear pattering in her pulse-beats. Dear heaven! The days of wanting him had become no more than a bitter memory, pushed out of sight, becoming more myth than reality, almost as if it had all been something that had happened to some other person, a very long time ago. Was it possible that he only had to touch her to set every cell in her body alight?

Without her being conscious of exactly when it had happened, he had released her arm, sliding his hands around her body, pressing her close to him, so close that they seemed to dovetail.

'I could make love to you until you begged for mercy,' he breathed against the heated skin of her cheek, his lips moving to close first one eyelid and then the other with kisses so light they were like the mere feathering of butterfly wings, trailing slowly down over her cheekbones to the lobe of her ear, nipping slowly and softly there before moving to the exposed length of her throat.

Her head thrown back, Fliss was aware of nothing but the heavy thumping of her heart, of the male scent of him, the soft warmth of his hair beneath the involuntary quest of her fingers. Then slowly, almost lazily, his mouth descended, his tongue feathering erotically against the warm valley between her breasts, his inescapable hands rotating her hips closer to his until she was made aware of the extent of his need.

A sheet of explosive sensation at the intimate contact drained the strength from her limbs, leaving her weak, melting into him, and he murmured throatily, his lips pushing aside the filmy barrier of her blouse, making her flesh ache with wanting . . .

'I could make love to you like this, and this . . . until you forget Gerald, forget the others who came before him, forget everyone but me . . .'

At the mention of Gerald's name, Fliss dragged her eyes open, blinking to clear the haze of desire. She remembered too well the way his voice could drop huskily, as it was doing now, the intimacy carried in the slow, sensuous tone almost shocking. His voice still had the power to make her melt, as his hands, his lips, had the power to turn her body to molten, weak desire. She groaned in anguish. Would she never learn?

Her body shaking now, she used both hands to push him away, catching the hot glitter of his eyes as she panted, 'Leave me alone. Just don't touch me!'

'Felicity——' his voice was thick '—don't try to deny you want me.'

'No!' Panic increased, hammering through her veins, her denial an instinctive travesty of the truth. She turned away, her eyes closed, fighting for the control which was the only thing that would ensure her safety.

'Who are you trying to fool?' He had regained his control with an ease that enraged her. It meant that his advances had been more cerebral than physical, and for some reason that hurt. It shouldn't do, of course, because what had just happened was merely a replay of what had happened four years ago. She should have expected it.

'You might try to fool yourself,' he insisted mockingly, 'but you can't fool me. I can recognise when a woman's sexually aroused.'

I just bet you do! she fumed inwardly, remembering Edwina and the languorous softness of her slender body as she had stirred in Leon's arms, sitting up slowly, voluptuously, her eyes dazed with the drugging aftermath of love.

Icily cold now, and very firmly in control, she turned to face him. She wanted to rake her nails over his mocking features. But she sacrificed that satisfaction, and gave him a tight smile, her passionate mouth parted over white, perfect teeth.

'For once in your life, Leon, you are wrong. I wanted to find out if your technique had improved over the years. It hasn't.' She lifted one shoulder minimally, then took her forgotten champagne from the table and drained the glass. It was as flat as she felt.

She had wanted to hurt him, as he had hurt her, but the victory was sour because, although her brain might scream a rejection, her body responded to his slightest touch with cataclysmic passion. The fact that she had been too young, too naïve to understand how to cope with the tumultuous feelings he aroused, had been responsible for her trepidation on their wedding night. Faced with his dark, devouring ardour—an ardour she now knew belonged to someone else—she had wanted to cry out that she loved him more than life, to abandon herself to him, to be everything he could want in a woman.

But inexperience and insecurity had prevented her from relaxing enough to respond to him at all, and now, in the light of what had happened, she thanked heaven for that. A wanton abandonment on her part, protestations of love, would, with hindsight, have been deeply humiliating because he had never wanted her at all.

She looked at him quickly, and saw the tight-lipped disgust on his face. The simmering quality of his long silence getting to her, she stated, 'You insisted on this farce of a so-called reconciliation; you also agreed that the marriage should continue in name only. So I suggest we stick to the ground rules if we're going to be able to live under the same roof without strangling each other.' She walked to the door, her body swaying in unconscious enticement. 'I'm going to bed. And, tell me,' her eyes met the dark glitter of his with an equanimity she was far from feeling, 'why did you go to such lengths to force me back? I have a right to know. You had been buying and selling Harlie's stock, and I wouldn't be surprised if you weren't behind Tim Ormond's uneconomic stipulations when it came to renewing the Martin and Bride's contract. You forced Harlie's to its knees, and then you delivered your ultimatum. Why?'

She was unimportant to him, she always had been, and Leon Draker didn't waste time on the unimportant things in life. So why did he want the marriage resumed? There had to be a reason, and the benefits would be stacked on his side.

'Don't you know why?' he asked edgily, advancing. There was an aura of leashed menace surrounding him; it made her heart race. But she didn't follow the tug of her senses and hurl herself from the room. She was tougher, now, than that.

'I wouldn't ask if I did.'

He stood tautly in front of her, and the space between them crackled with something invisible, electric.

She could feel the tension of it in her bones, in every fibre of her being, and it terrified her.

She was tall, but he towered above her, making her feel small and alone, and if he had reached out to touch her, told her that he wanted them to try again because he hoped they could forget the past and have something good, then, heaven knew, there was still something foolish enough, soft enough, left deep inside her to make her agree to anything he said.

'Then, I'll have to tell you.' His hands were bunched into the pockets of his expensively tailored cords, drawing attention to the sleek musculature of his thighs, and her eyes clouded as unwilling desire kicked to life inside her. She heard him say, 'I've found the married state to be very useful. That's why I never started divorce proceedings—though, heaven knows, I had grounds enough. Other women can't get too possessive if they know there's a wife in the background. But recently I've come up against someone who is possessive enough to be positively dangerous. She doesn't quite believe in your existence. Hence the need to have you on show. Satisfied?'

## CHAPTER SIX

FOR a moment she didn't believe him, and she stared at him from hazed eyes, shaking her head slowly to clear it. And then the import of his words hit her and she dragged in a breath, lashing out, 'You bastard!' her face paper-white.

'Probably,' he conceded drily. 'But what did you expect? You ran out on me, and I don't go a bundle on total celibacy. There were plenty of candidates willing to offer consolation.'

He turned away, leaving her leaning weakly against the door, and she closed her eyes and heard the rattle of a decanter against a glass.

'I just bet there were,' she commented rawly, gathering her resources. 'But didn't the divine Edwina object?' She had known he wouldn't live like a monk, she had had stark evidence of that when she had found his glamorous second cousin in his bed. But, in spite of that, she felt her insides clench with impotent fury.

'Jealous?' He lifted his glass to her in a mockery of a toast as he straddled the arm of a sofa, his eyes wicked, taunting.

'Go to hell!' she ground out viciously, then turned her head, hiding her expression.

'What about the men in your life?' he enquired sardonically. 'Don't try to tell me that what's sauce for the goose isn't sauce for the gander. I only know of two—the guy you left me for, and Gerald. But there must have been plenty in between. You learned that sensuality somewhere.'

'There were dozens in between!' she snapped, lying, her eyes flaring. He looked so cool, so laid-back, as if he held all the aces. And she wasn't going to tell him that no other man had ever come near her. Let him sweat a little!

'And, as you so rightly pointed out, what's good enough for you is good enough for me. So there will probably be dozens more!'

Her heart pumping erratically, she slipped out of the room, closing the door on the face of a man in a burning rage. The bones of his face were stark beneath his skin, giving him the look of a man whose monumental pride had been pricked, she thought with an inner shiver as she caught that glimpse of his terrible anger.

But she would go on pricking his pride, she vowed as she undressed for bed after carefully bolting the door. She would pay him back for what he had done to her, and would revel in every minute of it!

But, strangely enough, she cried herself to sleep, and the only time she'd shed tears of grief during the past four years had been when Netta had died.

She woke to sunlight streaming through the bedroom windows, and she stirred heavily, her head hurting, her eyes puffy with the tears that had seemed unstoppable. Another day to get through, she thought drearily as she showered, then bathed her face in icy water.

But she would manage it, she would cope. Pulling on a pair of jeans and a light sweater, she swept her hair back, and prayed that Leon would have already left for his suite of offices which, she guessed, would be situated directly beneath the penthouse.

And for once luck was with her. The apartment was silent, and a glance at the carriage clock in the main lounge told her it was nine-thirty.

Feeling like a child let out of school, she found her way to the kitchen. She had refused to eat last night, and was now ravenous. She would make tea and heaps of buttered toast and——

She stopped in her tracks, realised her mouth had dropped open, and snapped it shut. Standing in the centre of the technological wonder that was the penthouse kitchen was the oddest little man Fliss had ever laid eyes on. She had completely forgotten about Alfred Manley Spiker.

'Good morning, Mr Spiker.' She extended a long-fingered hand, smiling. Who could not smile when confronted by such a figure? He resembled an elderly garden gnome, decked in deepest mourning. 'I'm Fliss Draker.'

'I'm aware of who you are, madam.'

She was unprepared for the largeness of the voice which issued from the wizened little frame, or for the patent disapproval.

'I answer to the name of Spike,' he informed her with firm dignity, not a flicker of a smile on his untidy face to answer her own. 'When I served breakfast at eight, as is my custom, Mr Draker expressed the wish that you should be left to sleep.' He rolled up the long sleeves of his black cotton shirt, tweaked at his black waistcoat, and prepared to clean the silver cutlery laid out on the newspaper-covered central table. 'It would be helpful to know, madam, if you habitually sleep late and eschew breakfast.'

Fliss bit her lips on a giggle. She was being dismissed—firmly told that if she didn't show up for breakfast, at the time Spike had laid down for that meal, then she must go without.

But her stomach was rumbling with empty complaint, and gone were the days when she allowed herself to be dictated to.

'Carry on with with what you're doing,' she told the pedantic little man airily. 'I'm perfectly capable of making my own tea and toast.' Which she proceeded to do, with no help whatsoever from the disgruntled manservant. As she searched for a teapot and tried to figure out how the sci-fi kettle worked, she cast a fulminating glare at Spike's erect back. He was quite rigid with disapproval as he worked quickly and deftly over the silver. She wondered if he ruled Leon with the rod of iron with which he had attempted to beat her out of the kitchen, and decided he didn't. Leon would go his own way, and woe betide anyone who tried to stop him!

She recalled the softening of humour in his voice when he'd told her about Spike. He'd also said the man had been a boxer. That would account for the squashy nose and the untidy conformation of the ears—but it must have been half a century ago, and he must have fought at flyweight.

Finally, and thankfully, Fliss was able to leave the frigid atmosphere of the kitchen, carrying her tray of tea and toast, careful not to spill anything. She could well imagine the little man's wrath if she dropped so much as a crumb!

Eating alone in the solitary and impersonal splendour of the lounge, she felt herself to be immeasurably isolated. Leon, damn him, had dragged her away from all that was dear and familiar: her own small flat, her job, her friends. He had put her in prison. And, worse even than that, his reasons for wanting her back were as callous and calculated as they had been when he had married her.

Last night she had almost capitulated to her hateful captor. One word of gentleness from him, a word of regret, would have had her mindlessly agreeing to start again, to try for a true reconciliation. Her mouth curled mirthlessly. Without her realising it, there had still been a remnant of that younger, innocently gullible Fliss buried deep beneath the hardened shell of the woman she had fashioned out of the wreck of her marriage.

But last night's revelations had tolled the death knell for that unwanted remnant. There was no way he could ever be anything other than her enemy.

Her breakfast finished, Fliss carried the tray back to the kitchen. She was determined to get to know Spike better. If they were to be incarcerated in this apartment together, then they might as well be friends. Having one enemy perpetually at close quarters was bad enough.

He didn't look up as she entered the kitchen. His mouth was set in a tight, hard line. Fliss didn't like the look of that; it made her hoped-for attempts at peacemaking look impossible.

However, she asked, 'Do you need any help with that silver, Spike? There seems to be a great deal of it.' She put her used cup and plate in the sink, and slotted the tray back where she had found it, in a space between two of the many units.

Spike said, 'No, thank you, madam,' in a voice that could have squashed rocks.

But it had been a long time since Fliss had allowed herself to be squashed by anyone, so she came back, brightly but firmly, 'As you like. But I'm not used to being idle, and there must be something I can do to help around the place. Is Mr Draker coming back for lunch, by the way?' she added, because if the answer was yes she would make sure she was out.

'No, madam.' Spike stood up and went to the sink to wash his hands, removing her breakfast things as if they were contaminated. 'The master rarely lunches at home,' he informed her over the gush of water. 'And I do not require help with my duties. I have my routine, and the day I cannot follow it will be the day I retire. And, might I suggest, madam,' he turned the tap off and reached for a towel, facing her now, his eyes black in the surrounding soft web of wrinkles, 'that if you find idleness a burden, you expend your energies on something worthwhile—the happiness of your husband?'

Up until now Fliss had found his attitude amusing, if slightly aggravating. Now it was something else. Her eyes narrowing, she asked with misleading softness, 'What exactly do you mean?'

'Exactly what I said, madam.' His eyes flicked from hers to the gleaming silver on the table, lovingly polished, then back again, harder than before. 'I am devoted to your husband—I have good reason to be. And, with respect, I don't want to stand by and see him hurt again.'

A puzzled frown creased her brow. She didn't know what he was trying to say, and she didn't know whether to laugh at the antagonistic little man or threaten to fire him! But, in spite of his attitude, something about him impressed her; he wore his dignity like a cloak, covering his unprepossessing outward appearance, making him seem like an avenging angel.

'Would you mind elaborating?' she asked, hating the querulous squeak in her voice, and he nodded, simply, as if he understood her mood and, in a way, sympathised.

'I don't mean to sound antagonistic, madam, but I am concerned. I was told, by no less an authority than Mr Draker's mother, of the way you left him so early on in your marriage. And I have observed, at first hand, his tendency to drive himself too hard, as if nothing else mattered; the dark moods of sadness that come over him at times. And I saw the change in him when he told me you were returning. Quite simply, madam, he was happy, a changed man. His mother told me that you broke his heart four years ago, and I do not wish to see you break it all over again. He loves you very much, madam.'

Fliss couldn't believe she was hearing this! Her cheeks burned with heat, with outrage. Damn Annabel and her lies! Broken-hearted? Twaddle! The only emotion Leon would have experienced when she'd left him would have been relief.

Mistaking her crimson face for embarrassed remorse, Spike said, with a modicum of gentleness, 'But now you are back, older and wiser, perhaps. Wise enough to prefer the love of a gentleman such as your husband to any number of——' here his ugly face crimsoned to match her own as he coughed delicately and supplied '—a number of other male friends.'

She couldn't trust herself to speak. Face burning, she stalked out of the kitchen. Had Annabel told her filthy lies to anyone willing to listen? It was intolerable! She had a good mind to go right back, take that pompous little man by his scrawny throat and tell him that she had walked out on his beloved master—that paragon of all the gentlemanly virtues—simply and solely because she had discovered that he had married her to revenge himself on the woman he really loved. And that he had bedded that same woman right under her nose! And, furthermore, she was only back here, playing at being his wife, because it suited him at the moment to use her to keep his string of other women in their places—on their backs, no questions asked, no demands made! She wondered why she wasn't screaming.

She paced the confines of her bedroom many times, her arms wrapped tightly around her body, before she realised where she was and what she was doing. And, suddenly, she slumped, dropping down on to the bed.

None of this was Spike's fault. He had said he was devoted to Leon—though why, Fliss couldn't imagine! And so he had swallowed the lies Annabel had fed him. And why shouldn't he? And as for Leon loving her—well, she would be flat on her back, laughing her socks off if she'd felt in the mood for a joke. If he had looked pleased when he'd told Spike that the errant wife was returning, then it would have only been a reflection of his own relief—relief that he could flaunt her beneath the current mistress's nose.

She dragged a hand tiredly through her hair, scattering pins. She had never felt more alone, more friendless. She might as well be dead as immured here with a man who used her for his own loathsomely devious ends, and another who thought she was a common trollop!

Recognising the beginnings of self-pity, she hauled herself to her feet and forced herself over to the mirror, where she set about repairing the damage to her neat chignon.

Leon might be the devil in human guise, and he might have the upper hand right now, but that state of affairs wouldn't last longer than it took to get the Harlie-Draker merger finalised. And then her beloved husband wouldn't see her for dust! Only, this time round, she would take care to cover her tracks completely. This time round she wouldn't be a broken-hearted idiot, running blindly, leaving a trail any fool could follow. She had her wits about her now, and her emotions weren't involved. She would plan every move she made, well in advance.

And she wasn't friendless. Her friends were a couple of hundred miles away, that was all. Easily contactable by phone. And the first one she would contact would be Gerald. He cared about her, knew more about her than any other living soul—and he could give her details of that merger.

But her call to Gerald's office didn't have the comforting effect she had hoped for. After a few words with Amy Prentiss, his secretary—who had sounded oddly breathless and not at all her normal, chatty self—she had been passed on to Gerald, who had also sounded odd. Abstracted, Fliss thought, as if he had something pressing on his mind. After stiltedly acknowledging that he was well, that the date of the merger with Draker Electronics hadn't been set, Fliss decided she knew what was wrong.

'I'm sorry, Gerald, I shouldn't be taking up your time. I know how busy you must be. Why don't I phone you at home this evening, and we can have a good long natter?'

'I shan't be there. Sorry, Fliss.'

'No? Going somewhere exciting?' And that would be a minor miracle, she thought, her frown deepening. Something was wrong. Since Netta's death he had never gone out, apart from going into the office.

'Oh—well, I don't think it would interest you.' He sounded dismissive, and Fliss knew there had to be something on his mind. Something bad? Something he didn't want to worry her with? Reluctantly, she made her farewells, injecting a cheerful note with difficulty. Replacing the handset, she stared with vacant, unseeing eyes around the sparsely furnished room that was Leon's study, and his deep and rather beautiful voice came from the doorway.

'Who were you calling?'

If she'd been afraid of making waves, there were any number of lies she could have told: the hairdresser, an old schoolfriend—anyone. But she said, 'Gerald' and watched his face tighten, the lines around his mouth becoming more deeply incised, making his lips look cruel.

'I thought I'd told you to sever all connections there,' he said with chilling asperity, and she stood up from her perch on the corner of the big leather-topped desk and gave him the benefit of her most wintry smile.

'You may command the tide, O King, but you don't command me!' She eyed him with wary defiance. She would have liked to sweep out of the room—in fact, her feet were itching to do just that. But to gain the doorway she would have to pass too close to his tall and daunting person. And the last time she had attempted to sweep out on a telling one-liner she had reaped the bitter consequences. So she said, as dismissively as she could, 'According to the other He-Who-Must-Be-Obeyed,' she jerked her head in the general direction of the kitchen, 'you don't appear at lunchtime. So why are you here now?' She fiddled abstractedly with the blotter on his desk, pushing it this way and that, missing the flicker of amusement that lent silvery lights to his deep grey eyes.

'Don't tell me you've run foul of Spike as well!' He tossed his briefcase on to a leather club chair, moving, closing the space between them.

Fliss backed off, putting the width of the desk between them. Verbal sparring she could take, if she had to, but she couldn't take his nearness—it unnerved her, made her heart pound, her legs feel like jelly. 'As well?' she questioned, her tongue flicking nervously at the corner of her mouth.

'As well as me,' he qualified. 'I warned you that he rules the apartment absolutely. I hope you haven't injured his pride by giving him helpful household hints, or by offering to do the dishes!'

Fliss shrugged, pushing the blotter around some more—anything to avoid having to look at him, because his eyes were smiling now, his mouth relaxed, almost sensual, and that was something she didn't care to see. And not for anything would she tell him of her earlier brush with Spike. His ego was big enough as it was, without her inflating it even further by letting him know that the ex-flyweight was in his corner, ready and willing to do battle on his behalf!

'Spike's OK,' she answered airily. 'Apart from being two bricks short of a load—he seems to think you're some kind of deity.'

A low, velvety chuckle brought her skin out in goosebumps, but his following, 'I came to take you out to lunch—we've ten minutes before the cab arrives,' chased the weakness of awareness away and stiffened her backbone nicely.

'No, thanks. Go on your own.'

Her voice came out sounding sulky, and she hadn't intended that. She'd meant to sound casual, uninterested, but she must have given the impression of being the original dog in the manger because he said wearily, 'Don't be such a child, it doesn't suit you. Fetch your coat and try to behave in a civilised fashion for once.'

His remark implying her lack of sophistication had done it—that and the comforting adage about the impossibility of getting a horse to drink even after one had gone to the trouble of leading it to water. She would show him, at one and the same time, just how sophisticated and difficult she could be, she vowed as she effected a lightning transformation of her jeans-clad person.

Dressed in a discreetly expensive cream silk suit that did wonders for the remains of her Californian tan, she swept in a drift of Joy into the waiting cab.

'Not taking the car?' she enquired, brittly sweet.

'I intend to take a drink—wine, maybe a brandy—to take the afternoon off.' His easy reply as he settled his lean, elegant length beside her set her teeth on edge. Having to endure what would probably amount to a two-hour lunch with him was bad enough—let alone the rest of the day. But she wasn't going to let him know how his presence needled her; a picture of bored indifference was the one she had set out to portray.

'How nice.' She aimed a thin facsimile of a smile at nowhere in particular, then stiffened inside as she heard him speak again.

'We need to talk, Fliss, sensibly and seriously, and I thought a relaxed lunch might help set the tone.' He shifted slightly in his seat, making her uncomfortably aware of him, of the tangy aroma of the soap he used, of his body warmth stealing its invisible, invasive fingers across the small amount of space that separated them. She heard her heart pick up speed, and quickly turned to stare out of the window. He could still affect her—damn him! She knew exactly what he was—who better?—and yet he could still make her blood sing, her heart race, her flesh tremble. She must have rocks in her head!

'Fliss——' His voice was deep, velvet-smooth, and this was the second time he had used the diminutive she preferred. That alone was enough to make her questioning sapphire eyes turn to him—that and the way his hand captured hers, his hard-boned fingers cool against her palm.

A million sensations, all of them electric, sang through her veins at his touch, and to attempt to remove her hand, so she bemusedly assured herself, would merely result in that gentle handclasp tightening into talons of steel. So her hand lay passive within his, and she stared steadily at the back of the driver's head so that Leon wouldn't see how her eyes inevitably mirrored her reaction to the sensations he was creating.

'We've embarked on this second journey into marriage on the wrong foot entirely—and I admit I'm far more to blame for that than you. So can we start over, talk things out rationally, try to create an understanding—create a worthwhile relationship?'

The obvious sincerity in his voice took her breath away. It transported her to a place where good and wonderful things happened as surely as night followed day—a place where the impossible became, just for that moment, gloriously possible.

The eyes she turned to him were vulnerable, and her breath was sucked in on a gasp. The way his gaze moved slowly and sensuously from her suddenly hectic cheekbones to her softly parted lips affected her more than she had believed possible.

'Shall we try, Fliss?' The tone was husky, seducing her senses, the question merely rhetorical because he knew he had her in the palm of his hand. And that took her back, too—back four years in time to the day he had proposed to her. She had believed what she had thought to be his sincerity then, but events had all too quickly shown her how spurious it had been. She was not about to make the same mistake twice.

And yet—heavy raven lashes lowered to hide her eyes, masking her thoughts—and yet, it might be better if they did reach some kind of understanding. It could be weeks before she could walk out on him again. The merger still hadn't been finalised, and she would need to lay her plans very carefully this time, to ensure he couldn't track her down again. And weeks of in-fighting didn't appeal.

She had meant to be difficult over lunch, refusing to eat a thing, watching him eat with bored eyes, flicking the occasional ostentatious glance at her watch. In that way, she had figured, he would learn that he couldn't force her to do a single thing she didn't want to and, with luck, he wouldn't repeat the invitation.

But a truce of some sort did appeal, and when he said, 'Well?' the husky voice, the slight additional pressure on her fingers reminding her that she hadn't answered his question, she nodded.

'Yes, we'll talk things over,' she said, and wondered at his acting ability when she discerned a quiet kind of joy in the deep grey eyes.

'That's my girl!' The warm approval in his voice left her in no doubt that he thought he had her fooled, she decided cynically, wincing as he squeezed her hand until she thought her fingers might break. Then he released it and reached in an inner pocket.

'I notice you don't wear your wedding ring,' he said lightly—too lightly?—as he extracted a small, flat box. 'I imagine you threw it away, so I bought a replacement.'

She hadn't thrown the ring away, although that had been her original intention. But she hadn't been able to bring herself to do it, and it lay now, cocooned in cotton wool, at the bottom of her workbox.

In spite of herself, she was touched as he slid the plain gold band on to her finger, drawing in her breath as it was followed by a magnificent oval sapphire, set in heavy gold.

'I couldn't resist it—it reminded me of your eyes,' he explained with an offhandedness that didn't ring true. 'You didn't have an engagement ring before,' he added. 'I was in too much of a hurry to put the wedding ring in place.'

He sounded regretful, as well he might, Fliss thought waspishly. He hadn't been able to wait to have his revenge on Edwina, to produce a wife—to make Edwina suffer as he had suffered.

However, Fliss decided as they reached their destination and Leon ushered her between open smoked-glass doors flanked by bay trees in tubs, that was all in the past. This time around things were different because she was different, and she was perfectly willing to work with him towards some kind of understanding. Such a truce could make her hopefully short time with him at least tolerable. Anything else would be absurdly childish.

The restaurant he'd brought her to was discreetly expensive, and the fact that Leon used it often was obvious by the way he was warmly greeted and led immediately to the best table in the long, narrow gilt-and white-decorated room.

Laying aside the huge leather-bound menu after making her choice, she returned his smile across the white-linen-covered table. She was actually glad she had come, she acknowledged with inner amazement, more than pleased that the vicious in-fighting had stopped and that she had agreed that it should be so.

'You have pretty hands,' he told her when the waiter had moved away after serving their salmon mousse. 'The shape of the sapphire suits perfectly.'

'Thank you.' She felt herself colour with pleasure, very conscious of the heavy stone, of the simple gold band that encircled her finger. She would enjoy wearing the sapphire until the time came for her to leave. Absurdly, her thoughts were regretful, and for a moment she saw the day of their final parting not as a welcome goal, but as a penance—and not for the sake of a valuable ring, either!

And that was a dangerous attitude of mind, she warned herself, clamping her lips together and dropping her eyes as he feathered a fingertip across her flushed cheek.

They had to form a tolerable relationship. It was the only sensible, adult thing to do. And he had brought her here, to neutral ground, so that they could talk things out. But there would be no question of his talking her into accepting the restrictions he had put on her life for an indefinite period, or accepting this temporary marriage as a real one.

And with that firmly in mind, she reminded him, avoiding his eyes, 'So let's talk—that's why we came here, isn't it? I'm willing to try to find a way of making our situation tolerable.'

'Later. Let's simply relax and enjoy our meal. Then we'll go home and talk. And as for now, let's see if we can't try to become friends. Now, relax a little; drink your wine, Fliss.'

She lifted her glass obediently as her plate was removed and another, bearing the chicken and crayfish she had ordered, was placed before her. His lips had said one thing, but his eyes had told her that simple friendship was definitely not on his mind, and that made her feel very wary—but oddly excited, too. She put her glass down; her hand was shaking. And beneath her breastbone her heart was pattering, skidding around. She couldn't really believe that he wanted a true reconciliation, could she? And that wasn't what she wanted, was it?

For a brief, unguarded moment she didn't know what she did want. And, what was more frightening, more confusing than anything, was the way that the past four years had become blurred, out of focus, as if they had never really existed. It left her receptive, as vulnerable to him as she had been in those heady, rapturous days of her first and only love.

She dipped her head, not wanting him to read her thoughts before she had had time to analyse them herself.

'Darling!' The high-pitched, cultured accent cut into Fliss's muzzy thoughts, and she was aware of a cloud of cloying perfume, a presence. Lifting her head slowly, her eyes travelled the greyhound lines of a sleek ash-blonde. She was dressed in faultless taste, an older woman just behind her, more than likely her mother. 'I thought I might run into you here—if anywhere!'

'Charlotte——' Leon was on his feet, his smile urbane, his eyes bored. At least, Fliss thought it was boredom, until a gleam of something that looked suspiciously like unholy glee put her brain into overdrive.

Of course—a fool could work this one out! As she was introduced to Charlotte and her mother, Lady Flemmynge, Fliss's brain was clicking rapidly behind her social smile. She didn't need to see the sudden hazing of pain in Charlotte's green eyes to know that Leon had brought her here, given her those rings, with one objective in mind: to warn off a mistress who had become too demanding. Hadn't he already admitted that that was the only use he had for her? So why hadn't she been on her guard? Why had she allowed herself to be fooled by his spurious charm yet again?

Alone again, Leon said, 'Sorry about that. Let's eat, hmm?' and Fliss tossed her linen napkin beside her untouched meal and pushed her chair back.

'Enjoy it,' she remarked with a lightness she was far from feeling. 'I find I've lost my appetite.' And she walked away, tension keeping her spine rigid, making her sweat.

## CHAPTER SEVEN

A CAB cruised slowly round the corner into the side-street and Fliss stepped off the pavement, hailing it, oblivious of the stare of the liveried doorman who had welcomed them through those smoked-glass doors not half an hour earlier. She had no very clear idea of where she would go, she thought as the cab drew towards her. Hyde Park, perhaps, to walk this rage, this sense of betrayal out of her system.

Her decision made, she stepped forward, only to be nearly jerked off her feet as iron-hard fingers bit through the silk of her sleeve.

'The Draker building, Westminster,' he told the driver, his voice curt, and to Fliss, his mouth a grim line, 'Get in.'

'You certainly know how to foul things up,' he growled as the cab picked up speed. Speechless with rage, Fliss jerked her head round, staring at the swiftly moving traffic. Without even trying, he reduced her to a fireball of emotions, the poise and control that had been so hard-won over the past four years reduced to a risible memory. Her whole body was quivering, her teeth clamped together with tension, making her jaw ache.

He was wrong. He was the one who fouled things up—deliberately, and with a callousness that took her breath away. She should have learned her lesson after learning precisely why he had married her in the first place. But no—her mouth twitched with self-disgust—

oh, no! Twice within twenty-four hours she had come within a whisper of admitting to herself that she cared about the bastard! Twice! And, idiot that she was, she had actually been touched by the gesture of affection he had made when he had given her those rings, his seemingly sincere desire to get this second attempt at marriage on to a better footing.

Breathing raggedly, she twisted the heavy sapphire off her finger and tossed it in his direction, not caring where it landed. Bought it because it matched her eyes! Like hell! Would she never learn? The wedding ring followed.

From the corner of her eye she saw him pocket the rings, and defeatedly admitted that her gesture had come too late. The rings had served their purpose. The jewel, particularly, was unmissable and would have effectively underscored the simplicity of his introductions—'Charlotte, meet my wife, Felicity.' She would never forget the pain in the blonde's eyes. Never.

Outside the Draker building, her legs threatened to buckle. Only his grip on her arm kept her upright. She risked a look at his face as he turned from paying the driver, and what she saw there made her stomach heave. He looked as if he would like to throttle her!

He marched her towards the private lift, and, once inside the claustrophobic metal box, she began to shake again, dreading the interview ahead of her which would now take the place of the promised 'friendly talk'. She needed time to get herself together, to cancel out the mind processes that had confusingly suggested, for a brief span of time, that he wasn't really her enemy at all—that things could, if they both worked at it, be different.

As the lift moved upwards at what seemed to her to be a snail's pace, he took a step towards her, and she snapped, 'Don't touch me!'

'I don't want to,' he answered grimly, his face set. He was breathing rapidly, as if he'd been in a fist fight, but he said, levelly enough, 'I'm stopping off at my office—at least there's logic in project projections. You can carry on up to the apartment.'

Her chin lifted and she glared right back at him, quelling the quite perverse feeling of disappointment that weighted her heart. She didn't actually want him to stick with her, did she? She couldn't want to take part in yet another brutal slanging match, could she? She couldn't be that crazy!

'And if I don't want to be shut up all afternoon in that—that prison? It bores me to death!' she flashed.

'Tough,' he commented drily. 'But as a prison it must come with a five-star rating.' He was standing squarely in front of the doors, his hands bunched into the pockets of his sleek grey trousers, his broad shoulders dismissive. And as the doors slid open he was out, no backward look. A man in a vile temper.

Moments later, stepping out into the apartment, her mind quietening just a little, she reflected on that anger. It was so real she could have reached out to touch it. Yet it made no sense.

True, she must have caused a few raised eyebrows when she'd walked out on him and her untouched meal. But he had panache enough to handle a little thing like that. He could take in his elegant stride things that would have made a less assured man crumple up with embarrassment. Besides, he had done what he had said he would do—used her and their marriage to warn off a possessive mistress. He should be rejoicing, not blazingly, furiously angry!

She was still uptight when Spike announced from the lounge doorway that dinner was served. Turning from her solitary station at the wall-width window, she walked quickly through the room on her way to the dining-room next to the kitchen, almost colliding with Leon as he emerged from his bedroom. A cursory glance over his black-shirt-and-trousers-clad figure was all the acknowledgement she gave him as she stalked on ahead. And what Spike thought about the separate bedrooms they occupied made her mouth twitch mirthlessly. It would be quite obvious that she was not taking her task of making her husband 'happy' to its full conclusion, and she guessed she'd be in for more of the cold-shoulder treatment from that direction!

Not that she cared, she told herself firmly. Spike's little lecture this morning would have been laughable, except for the fact that her mother-in-law—having accomplished what she'd set out to do—was now telling all and sundry that the break up was entirely Fliss's fault! And, in any case, she reminded herself, she wouldn't be here so very much longer.

'Thank you, Spike,' Leon commented as the little servant helped them both to a richly aromatic game casserole. 'This looks wonderful, as always.'

But, wonderful or not, Leon ate little, Fliss noted. She forced herself to eat some of the food, but the atmosphere between them was enough to kill the keenest appetite.

'You said you were bored,' Leon remarked at last, leaning back in his chair, watching from beneath enigmatically lowered lashes as Fliss poured coffee from the pot Spike had left. 'You've barely been here for twenty-four hours.'

'Twenty-four minutes would have been enough to bore me to tears,' Fliss came back smartly. The long afternoon had given her time to recover from the aberration of softening towards him. He was firmly printed on her mind as a swine of the first water—for now and all time. She would not make the same mistake again. 'I'm used to using my brain, keeping occupied—not being cooped up in a sterile, expensive hutch!' She put his coffee in front of him gracelessly, and took her own to the opposite end of the room, where she stared belligerently at one of the paintings on the panelled walls.

No matter how hard she promised herself to remain calm, to revert to being the cool, collected young woman she had been before he had erupted back into her life, she was finding it almost impossible.

'It's largely up to you to make the situation less sterile, Fliss.' He had come to stand behind her, without her hearing him move. She flinched, the coffee-cup rattling on its saucer as his hands lightly touched her shoulders and fell away again. 'I'm willing to do what I can,' he added, his voice low, husky with something she didn't want to recognise.

She felt his breath feather the skin on her nape, making her throat tighten. How could she allow herself to be affected by him like this? she thought with violent self-disgust as he reached round her and took the cup and saucer from her flaccid hands, putting them down on a side table and turning her to face him.

Loathing herself, she tugged away, dislodging his hands from her shoulders. Dropping, his hands brushed against her breasts and fire licked through her, making her close her eyes as if in agony.

'How would you like to work for me? I guarantee you wouldn't have time to be bored.' His voice was lightly teasing, and there were pinpricks of silvery laughter in the deep grey of his eyes. It was as if he had recognised the sensations that had almost crippled her at that accidental, erotic touch.

'How do you mean?' she managed, suspiciously. She was shaking inside. He wasn't touching her now, but he didn't need to. His presence alone was enough to pull her poise into tatters.

'I had a word with personnel. We could find you a place in PR—no problem at all.'

No, no problem at all for a firm such as his to come up with what would probably amount to being a nothing of a job—just to keep the boss's wife from being bored, she thought acidly as she edged away from him and reseated herself at the table. She didn't want to be near him, didn't want to have to cope with the conflicting emotions his nearness provoked.

'No, thanks.' Almost, she could have been grateful that he had second guessed her need to be occupied, had gone to the trouble to find a position within his company. Almost, she could like him for that. But she had to be tougher with him, tougher with herself. 'I do have some standards. I won't work for a rogue and a schemer.'

He had been walking back towards the table, too, but he stopped dead in his tracks at that—very still, dark, menace in every tautly drawn line of his body.

'I am doing my damnedest to be patient,' he ground out. 'And, after this morning's tantrum, I think I deserve a medal for even trying.' His shapely hands clenched into fists at his sides. 'So what the hell do you mean by that snide remark?' The words were like a whiplash.

Danger surrounded him like an aura. It would be easy enough to be terrified by the powerful, still man. But Fliss wouldn't let herself be—at least, she wouldn't demean herself by showing fear.

She was quivering inside, but she took a peach from the bowl on the table and began to slice it neatly as she elucidated, her tone almost conversational, 'The only way you could get me to agree to come back to you was through Gerald and his company. Make Harlie's vulnerable, and you make me vulnerable. Simple—for a man who deals dirty.' She ignored his angry hiss of indrawn breath, her eyes flicking over his still, tautly held body with cool blue contempt. 'Simple for a man who means to buy steadily and heavily into Harlie's stock, and then sell and sit back and gloat while the share value dropped.'

'So——' He resumed his seat opposite her, and he wasn't angry now—in fact, he was almost smiling, and that unnerved her. 'So you disapprove of that type of manipulation?' he asked, his husky tone sending shivers down her spine. 'You're too moralistic. Besides, I had big stakes to play for. And I don't mean Harlie's.'

Fliss ignored that. She knew only too well what he'd wanted—a wife, living under his roof again, a wife he could use to keep other women at a safe distance. He was callous, disgusting!

'And, just to make sure, you bribed Tim Ormond to lose the Martin and Bride contract,' she accused hotly, putting down her fruit knife and pushing the unwanted peach slices away. 'I discovered how he'd been operating—making conditions of sale so unviable that our main stockists refused to renew the contract. It didn't take me long to put two and two together. There was no reason Tim Ormond would do such a thing unless he'd been offered a bribe he couldn't refuse,' she told him with scathing logic.

There was an ominous silence and, at last, risking a look from between sweeping raven lashes, she saw grim humour paint his face—not the expected rage at having been found out in one more piece of devious dealing. Her heart picked up its beat, hammering beneath her heaving breasts. He looked devilish, full of dark intent. Fire burned behind the smoky grey of his eyes, and she was uncomfortably aware of the hard, vital body beneath the casual black clothes.

'Have you finished?' he enquired silkily, and Fliss wiped the juice from her fingers on her snowy napkin and pushed back from the table, deliberately misunderstanding. Discretion, and all that, she told herself wryly.

'Quite, thank you. It was a superb meal. Goodnight.'

But he was much too quick for her, and his fingers clamped around her wrist, making her gasp as hard bone bit against soft skin.

'Let me go!' she said shortly, playing down the fear that made her eyes glitter, her breath coming in raw tatters.

'Not until I've finished,' Leon retorted, capturing the hand she instinctively raised to ward him off, increasing the pressure on both wrists now, until she could have cried aloud with the pain of it. Unshed tears pricked at the back of her eyes—burning shameful tears—and she bit down hard on her lower lip to stem the flow. 'Stop fighting me, Fliss,' he commanded, his voice deep, hypnotically sexy. 'As I said earlier, we need to talk, to put things straight.'

But the look in those devilish dark grey eyes warned her that talking was not what he had in mind right now, and as he drew closer, slid his arms around her, she instinctively stiffened, her eyes wary.

'You are beautiful, Fliss.' He moulded her resisting body closer to his with an ease that terrified her, repeating, 'So beautiful,' his sensual mouth a brand against the fine skin of her temple. His hands were shaping her body with wicked expertise, and response kicked to life deep within her—logic, common sense, flying out of the window beneath his assault on her senses.

Her blood pounding, her mind skittered uneasily as it tried to alert her body's defence mechanism, but her body had a will of its own, and was heeding nothing but the fatal chemistry that had inexorably drawn her to him four years ago... And drew her still.

Trembling, she drew her head back as she looked up at him. His eyes were smoky, hazed with desire, and his hands moved to her head, gently positioning her mouth to receive his kisses—lightly given, but devastating—tasting her again and again. His splayed hands twined deftly through her hair, removing pins so that it fell, a glossy raven waterfall around her shoulders.

'Fliss——' Her name was torn from him before he bent his head and plundered her lips again in a kiss that was mind-blowingly passionate, as if his control had left him. Taking her with him on a journey into pure sensation, he pressed her softly voluptuous body to the lean, mature strength of his, and she responded with a wildness of her own, uncaring of the past, the future, because now was all that mattered, these electrifying sensations the only reality her spinning mind could absorb.

'Ahem!' It was a very loud, staged cough, and Fliss froze in Leon's arms, felt his mouth reluctantly drag away from hers, heard the soft hiss of his breath as he swore softly.

'I came to clear, sir, and to ask whether you need anything else for tonight.'

'Nothing more, Spike.' Leon's voice could have frozen a lava flow; he didn't need to actually come out and say he viewed the servant's interruption as a crass, insensitive blunder.

Flushed, breathing raggedly, Fliss caught sight of Spike's ugly face, wreathed in smiles. And he smiled more broadly as he moved about the table, collecting dishes, noting that neither had eaten more than a mouthful or two.

That satisfied smile—and the lines of frustration around Leon's beautifully sculpted mouth—reminded Fliss with awful clarity of what she had been doing. She had been showing him—heaven help her!—exactly how malleable she was. One caress, one kiss, and she was putty, a creature he could manipulate at will. A silly, mindless puppet!

Her legs shaking, she fled the room, nausea making her stomach burn. Gaining the relative safety of her bedroom, she bolted the door and sat heavily on the edge of her bed, staring into the darkness.

## CHAPTER EIGHT

A GREY little wind whipped the pewter waters of the Thames, and Fliss turned away, walking along the Embankment. Shivering slightly, her face pale, she dug her hands into the pockets of her white wool blazer and increased her pace. Spike would have dinner ready, she thought without enthusiasm, a place set for one at the elegant dining-room table, a delicious meal she wouldn't be able to eat.

At this rate—walking for hours every day, barely picking at her food—she would soon lose her 'vulgar curves' and become as greyhound-thin as the thoroughbreds which were so exactly to Leon's taste. A wry smile flickered over her mouth; she didn't want him to find her attractive—most assuredly she did not. It had been bad enough trying to fend off his embraces—those kisses and caresses that had only been given in an attempt to bind her with his magic—without him finding her attractive enough to actually enjoy it!

He had probably feared she might do another runner before her usefulness had served its purpose—Harlie's or no Harlie's. And so he had tried to bind her to him, arousing her sexual need as only he knew how, and she—fool that she was—had been only too eager to help him!

Still, Spike had saved her from herself. He had thwarted Leon's plans—for the moment. And Spike's timely interruption had had other compensations, she reminded herself. The little man quite obviously believed the evidence of his eyes, believed she was throwing herself wholeheartedly into the so-called reconciliation, and his attitude had changed. No more grim-faced disapproval. He couldn't do enough for her now. All this last week, while Leon had been away, Spike had fussed over her like a mother hen with a single chick.

It was a beautiful morning. The grey skies of yesterday were gone, and Fliss woke early, dressed in a pale lemon sun-dress, and decided to spend the day at Kew Gardens.

Goodness knew how long Leon would stay away, she thought with a tinge of exasperation as she brushed her long black hair and plaited it into a single, heavy braid. The longer the better, she thought, wondering if she really meant that. A business trip, he'd explained tersely as he'd stepped into the lift on the morning after Spike had interrupted his attempted seduction.

The metal doors had closed and she'd heard the muted whoosh of the descending lift, and had thought, 'Who do you think you're kidding, mister?' A little much-needed relaxation with an accommodating mistress was more like it—after his distasteful and unsuccessful efforts with her!

She knew she should have taken this week's respite as the ideal opportunity to plan her moves for when the time came to leave him. But she had been strangely restless, unable to settle her mind to anything, finding physical activity the only answer.

So, today she would go to Kew, and tomorrow she would definitely sit down and decide where to go and what to do when the merger was finalised and Harlie's safe. One thing was certain, she decided grimly as she made her way to the dining-room where Spike would have her toast and coffee waiting, next time he wouldn't find her—not if he searched for a million years!

'Good morning, Fliss.'

Wide-eyed with shock, she stared at the unwelcome sight of her husband enjoying what appeared to be a lavish breakfast. He was wearing a casual shirt in gun-metal grey, and narrow-fitting black denims. And there was a smile on his lean, handsome face as he asked, 'Miss me?'

Seeing him so unexpectedly had addled her brain, she decided fuzzily, gulping to relieve the sudden tension that had closed her throat. She felt cold, and hot, and her stomach churned, flopping about—and that was ridiculous!

'Like a boil on the backside!' she grated inelegantly, relieved that she had found some form—albeit crude—from the mish-mash of her emotions.

'Have some breakfast.' Leon smiled expansively, obviously not put out by her greeting. 'And stop griping. It's a lovely day, so why spoil it?'

Fliss sat at the table, carefully, as though the chair were made of spun glass, simply because there didn't seem to be anything else to do. She couldn't understand why he was smiling, looking so completely relaxed. The woman he'd been with must have been quite something, she thought sourly. Because, after the greeting she'd given him, she would have expected him to be hurling the coffee-pot at her head, not pouring from it, handing her a cup.

'Drink it up, it might improve your mood,' he advised, his dark grey eyes lazily amused. 'And what have you been doing with yourself all week?'

He's treating me like a backward child, she thought rancorously, waving away the china toast-rack he was pushing towards her.

'What's more to the point, what have you been doing?' She managed to eject a wealth of cynicism into the enquiry, and was pleased to see his eyes harden, his expression grow guarded. So, he had been with some woman! And she had caught him out! But, annoyingly, that pleasure turned rapidly to pain—a deep, deep, tearing pain, the like of which she had never believed herself capable of feeling again, and she said tightly, 'Business, you *said*,' letting him know that she didn't believe that, not for one moment.

He sighed. 'That's right, business.' Then, softly, leaning back and crooking one arm over the back of his chair so that the silky fabric of his shirt pulled taut across his hard-muscled chest, 'We're going to have to talk, Fliss. And today I've given myself a holiday, so now is as good a time as any to start. Wouldn't you say?'

'I don't know what there is to talk about.' She knew she sounded surly, but she couldn't help that. She was having difficulty with her breathing. His shirt was open at the neck, and his relaxed pose revealed more bronzed skin than she cared to see, revealed the crisp dark body hair that she knew arrowed right down over the flat planes of his stomach . . .

Quickly, she dropped her eyes and began stirring her coffee and he said lazily, 'Then let me toss something into the melting pot for starters—I may have done some manipulating when it came to forcing the

Harlie's board to go for a merger, but I had never, and I repeat—*never*—laid eyes on Ormond before the day I went to his office to go through his records. It only took a glance through his files and a couple of phone calls to tell me that Ormond had been deliberately trying to sabotage Harlie's. If Gerald had done the necessary digging, he would have found out that Ormond's uncle is the head of Harlie's closest rival, Tech-Elec—and, with all respect,' his voice took on a withering tone, 'if you had been on the ball you would have suspected that something was wrong with his department when sales started to slump to such a degree. You should have been able to pin down the person responsible. I don't stoop to using bribery, Fliss.'

'No—only to using blackmail on a woman!' she yelped, stung to fury by the very fact that he was right! Gerald had been so pleased to have an old friend contact him in those dark days following Netta's death that he would have hired Tim Ormond even if he'd been an imbecile! And she—well, it had taken her a long time to look beyond the irritation of Tim's lengthy absences from the office, his lavish expense-account lunches, to the real meat of the matter. As no doubt Ormond had planned!

But hearing it from her enemy's lips made it harder to live with, and she made to get up, to leave the room, but something in his eyes, something she had never seen there before, something remarkably like humility, stopped her as he said, 'And that's precisely what we have to discuss. This so-called blackmail you keep throwing in my face.'

'So-called?' she repeated loudly, her fine black eyebrows shooting up at the sheer effrontery of the man, two bright splashes of colour on her cheeks making her eyes look huge.

'Fliss—I don't usually do business that way——' He captured her hands as they lay bunched into fists on the smooth beige table-cloth, his touch warming her, his fingers coaxing hers to relax until her hands opened, nestling quietly within his.

He could so easily reach her on the physical plane, she thought bitterly, yet in every other respect they were miles apart.

'But, you see, my dear, you left me no option——'

'May I clear now, sir?' Spike trotted in with a tray that looked almost as big as himself. 'Or do you require more coffee? It's a fine morning, is it not?' He was beaming, and Fliss didn't give herself top marks for guessing why. His beloved master had returned, and the errant wife had clearly mended her ways and was holding his hands across the breakfast-table in the most satisfactory way. Billing and cooing!

Fliss dragged her hands from Leon's immediately, hearing the edge of impatience as he agreed, 'Yes, a lovely day,' and then said to Fliss, 'Shall we go through to the lounge and carry on from where we left off?'

Spike obviously thought that was a great idea. A little more billing and cooing was just what his master needed—Fliss could practically read his thoughts—but routine was routine, and she could have yelped with laughter when Spike proved her right, saying with obvious regret, 'Today is the day I give the apartment a thorough vacuuming—starting directly after breakfast, sir. I'm sorry, sir.' But she didn't have the opportunity to display her mirth, because Leon was on his feet, knocking over his chair, his mouth a tight line of frustration.

'Can't a man have any privacy in his own home? Fliss——' In one sharp movement he reached out for her, dragging her to her feet, his fingers inescapable, hard. 'Get your things, we're spending the day out!'

And that wasn't such a bad idea, she decided as she fetched her handbag from her bedroom. She had been looking forward to spending the day at Kew—well, as much as she'd been capable of looking forward to anything during this last week. With Leon the outing would be infinitely more agreeable. He could be an excellent companion when he chose, and he could hardly start yelling at her or trying to seduce her in the middle of Kew Gardens, where there would undoubtedly be thousands of other people intent on making the most of the weather.

'I'd thought of going to Kew,' Fliss said serenely as she fastened her seat-belt, relaxing back against the leather upholstery and admiring the competence with which he eased the powerful vehicle from the car park beneath the prestigious Draker building and into the flow of westbound traffic.

She flicked a glance at his profile, not put out by his silence because there really was nothing to say. No amount of talk, discussion, whatever, could change a situation which was, in her opinion, quite clear-cut and patently intolerable. He looked quite amazingly relaxed, but, despite that, he exuded his unique brand of sexual chemistry; it made her whole body tingle. She shivered.

'Not cold, surely? Shall I cut the air-conditioning?'

She shook her head, not looking at him, and he imparted, 'Kew can wait. I've somewhere quieter in mind. It won't take much longer than a couple of hours to get there.'

A couple of hours? Cooped up with him, the tension that always electrified the air between them growing inevitably tighter with every second that passed. How in the name of sanity was she going to stand it?

'Why don't we just relax a little and take up from where we were before Spike routed us?'

The question was casually put—there was even a smile in his voice, she noted bitterly. He could afford to relax, to smile, to take all this in his stride. Everything was going exactly as he wanted it to, he had the upper hand—and he knew it. She was hog-tied, certainly until the merger was finalised—and for much longer if he had his way. And, of course, there was the added bonus—he could turn her into a mindless fool, just by touching her. And he knew that, too.

'Well?' he prompted quietly, and she unconsciously shook her head, staring out of the window at the rows of neat, suburban houses. She was too tense to say a word. Two hours of this—and if they started rowing now she wouldn't be able to stand it. Already her breath had solidified in her throat, making her heart hammer.

'Why don't you tell me what you're thinking now, for instance? What your thoughts are on our marriage? We could go on from there.'

They were out of the built-up area now, and the powerful car was moving at speed, but totally under his control. But then, he was always in control, wasn't he? And what did he want her to say? That she wanted him to make love to her, that she wanted the past wiped out, their marriage to become the multi-faceted thing—tender, companionable, caring, passionate, fulfilling—that she had dreamed of in her youth and innocence? But the past couldn't be wiped out, she knew that, so dreams of the perfect marriage weren't permissible or wise. And if she told him that, under the circumstances, she wanted to be half a world away from him, never to have to see him again, he would believe it and begin to take extra precautions to ensure she didn't escape him until he was ready to see her go.

Again she wordlessly shook her head. She had nothing useful to say to him on the tangled subject of their hopeless marriage. She couldn't think why he was so anxious to chew it over, either. Perhaps it gave him a feeling of power.

'You never give, do you?' he stated tersely. 'You never give anything of yourself. Ask yourself how many times you have truly shared, told me what you were thinking, feeling.' There was a rough edge to his voice, and she knew it wasn't anger. She risked a quick look at his taut, chiselled profile, her eyes widening to deep blue pools as he told her rawly, 'Damn it all, Fliss, you're my wife and I don't even know the first thing about your family. They're all in California—that's the excuse you gave for not inviting them to our wedding. And that's all I do know. So tell me about them, about your early life. Were you a tear-away at school, or a bookworm? Were you a mother's darling, or the bane of the neighbourhood? You know, for all you ever said about your people, you might have been found, at the age of eighteen, under the mythical gooseberry bush!' He took his eyes from the road then, his mouth tilting warmly in a way that searingly reminded her of those earlier days—those stingily few days before their marriage when all the world had seemed wonderful, and he the most wonderful thing in it.

'Do you have brothers and sisters?' he questioned. 'In the past, whenever I introduced the topic, you looked the other way and changed the subject.'

She smiled just a little, looking down at her hands which were curled in her lap. He was right, of course. She had never been able to talk about her early life—or only to Netta and Gerald, and then only because she had been particularly alone and vulnerable after the break up of her farcical marriage. Her parents' attitude towards her had produced a crippling sense of inferiority, making her feel of no value. If her own parents had been unable to love her, then how could she expect anyone else to?

Besides, before they'd married they had talked—really talked—very little. They had progressed almost immediately from the language of strangers to the language of love. And where he had led, she had followed, bewildered but enchanted by his tender words, delighting in them quietly, too unsure of herself to give voice to feelings that were deeper and more devastating than she could explain, even to herself.

But things were different now. Gerald and Netta's fondness for her, their faith in her, coupled with her recent trip to America, had cleared her vision. She was mature now, sure of her own worth. So, yes, she could tell him now.

Staring ahead, her eyes on the road, on the heat haze that shimmered above the tarmac, she said unemotionally, 'My mother left my father and me when

I was a few months old. Father never spoke about her, but when I went back to live with Father again a neighbour enlightened me. I must have been five, or thereabouts.'

'Back to live with him?' The glance he spared her was puzzled, and Fliss shrugged lightly, relieved, in a way, that she could now talk to him like this and not feel the pain, the uncertainty. It meant she was over that particular trauma.

'When Mother left us he didn't want me, either. He farmed me out with a married cousin of his. But he remarried when I was just gone four years old, and had me back. Not, I gather, because he and his new wife were anxious to make a home for me, but because Betty—his cousin—wanted rid of me.'

'And it was then you found out what had happened to your mother?'

'That's right. This neighbour was a ghastly old woman—the type who believes in calling a spade a spade, and speaking her mind, regardless of who might get hurt.' She laughed wryly, softly. 'Well, she felt it her duty to inform me that my mother left because she couldn't bear being tied down by a child. She was a singer, and she put her career first. She didn't earn enough to employ a full-time nanny, and neither did Father, and they were always rowing—according to the neighbour—so she cut and ran. I never found out if she made it to the top or not. We never heard from her.'

'Did you check up on all that?' he asked quietly. 'That woman, the neighbour, could have got it wrong. Outsiders rarely see others' marriages clearly.'

'Eventually. I brooded about it for a year or two. Father was a remote man—at least where I was concerned. I didn't find it easy to talk to him. But I plucked up courage a few years later, and he told me that, yes, it was true, and said he didn't want to hear my mother's name mentioned again. So I didn't, and neither did anyone else. I stayed on with Father and Louise, his new wife, and things went from bad to worse.'

'Back up a little,' he commanded. 'What was life like with your father's cousin, Betty?'

'So-so.' Fliss raised one shoulder, noting how white were the knuckles of the hands that gripped the steering-wheel. But her mind was back in time, objectively viewing an unkempt little girl whom nobody wanted. 'She was never unkind, not really. But she did have four children of her own, and the house was small. Looking back, I can see that I must have been a drain on already strained patience. I don't remember a great deal about those early years—just that Father never came to see me, although he did send money for my keep. I didn't even know what he looked like. And I remember the gladness on Betty's face when she told me I'd be going back to my father.'

'And then?'

'What would you expect?' Fliss smiled bleakly. They were driving through open countryside now, along deep narrow lanes, through tiny hamlets. She would have preferred to concentrate on the scenery. However, she continued.

'By the time Louise produced twin boys I was five and ready to go to school. At the time I equated starting school with their desire to get me out of the way. They idolised the twins, and what little attention they'd previously given me disappeared after they were born. I suppose I must have resented them because my father loved them, and not me. As far as he was concerned, I was a nuisance and an unwelcome reminder of his first disastrous marriage. And Louise, well, I was just a chore she'd taken on when she'd married Father. I couldn't understand why they never cuddled me as they cuddled the boys, why they never let me play with them. But I can understand it now, because by then I'd become a ghastly child—wilfully disobedient, prone to throwing tantrums at the drop of a hat——'

'Attention-seeking,' Leon supplied. 'Poor scrap.' He sounded as if he really cared, felt for that prickly, lonely child. But Fliss knew that was nonsense. To him, this soul-baring was a marginally better way of passing the time than total silence.

'Absolutely,' she agreed. She'd worked that one out for herself! 'I became so unmanageable that, by the time Louise had had her daughter and I was eight, they decided boarding school was the only proper place for such a disruptive creature!' She could smile about it now, those schooldays where her antisocial behaviour had been knocked out of her, the lonely holidays spent in the company of some well-meaning paid childminder—rarely, very rarely, at home. The deep sense of shame in feeling herself unlovable.

'And they went to the States—when?' he asked, pulling off the quiet country lane on to the tiny car park of a timbered inn.

'When I was seventeen. I was invited to go along, but I hadn't lived with them for nine years. And nothing had changed, I was still the outsider. Besides, I'd begun a secretarial course, shared a flat with another girl, had started to make some kind of life of my own. I decided to stay in England.' And that's where you came in, she thought tartly. And the less said about that, the better! 'Is this where you had in mind?' she asked the obvious, just for something to say to change the subject, because at this point in her story they came to dangerous ground. She unfastened her seat-belt and gave him a tight, meaningless smile. She didn't know why he had brought her here, and, suddenly, she didn't care.

During the drive—and probably due to all she had told him—her mind had changed gear. Magically, the tension seemed to have gone, and she got out of the car and stretched her stiff limbs, lifting her face to the glare of the sun, filling her lungs with clean, country air.

'We'll have an early lunch and then walk, unwind.' He locked the car and came to stand at her side, and he said quietly, 'Why didn't you tell me any of this before? Years ago, when we first met?'

'Should I have done?' she countered easily, her sapphire eyes finding his serious grey gaze. 'Would it have made the slightest difference to the way things turned out?' She knew it wouldn't have done—nothing could have altered his reasons for marrying her.

But he said, 'Quite probably. It would have explained many things—helped me to understand that vast inferiority complex that made it impossible for you to accept your position at Feathergay, to understand the way you froze whenever I tried to make love to you. You had never been given love, and so you found it difficult to give—or, at least, to show. You believed you were unlovable. It had been programmed in you since you were born.'

He looked thoughtful, the bright sunlight making his eyes look silver, and Fliss thought bitterly, How astute! then pushed the acid thought away.

There was no point in bitterness; the past was behind her, and it would stay that way. Their marriage had been a failure because he had married her for all the wrong reasons, and now he was using her to fob off any woman who might get too emotionally dependent on him. When it ended, as end it must, she would get a divorce.

And he had talked of love; that had to be a joke. What could he know about it? He had never been in love, laid himself open to that hellish vulnerability. Or perhaps he had truly loved Edwina, she thought tiredly, and after that, all else was lust. A kind of using, as he was using her now.

He was still watching her closely, and it made her feel uncomfortable. If he probed too deeply into her earlier life, he might just discover how much she had loved him at the time of their marriage. And that would never do.

Giving him a brisk smile, she began to walk across the gravel to the open door of the inn. 'If we're going to have lunch, let's have it,' she said.

He made a visible effort to pull himself together—as if his mind had been far away on a different plane—and fell in step beside her, his smile warm, his hand on the small of her back, burning her through the thin cotton of her sun-dress. But, strangely, she welcomed the contact. She felt closer to him now than she had ever done. Maybe their talk in the car had opened the way for an easier relationship. She didn't know, but she wasn't going to fight the new affinity she suddenly felt with this man. Just for today, she would look on him as her friend. Tomorrow would be soon enough to recognise him again for the enemy that he was.

## CHAPTER NINE

THE sun had dropped low in the sky, but Fliss didn't feel chilly. She came awake slowly, savouring each sensation, not actually opening her eyes because she knew he was still sitting beside her. She could feel his body heat. At last she placed the source of her own warmth. Leon had taken a wool rug from the car, after lunch when they'd set out for their walk. But they hadn't used it to sit on, because the grassy bank they'd found, overlooking the small lake he'd brought her to, had been crisply dry.

So he must have covered her with the rug as she slept, making sure she kept warm when the sun lost its strength and a breeze had sprung up from the lake. She could smell the lake now, the trees that crowded round it, the masculine scent of his no-nonsense soap, of silk against warm male skin.

She stirred then, her body relaxed and languorous beneath the covering of plaid wool, and she turned her head to look up at him from slumbrous sapphire eyes.

'Pleasant dreams?' he asked softly, a smile in the silver-flecked dark grey eyes. 'You must have been exhausted; you haven't stirred for hours.'

To be truthful, her dreams had been disturbing rather than pleasant. Erotic fragments, featuring Leon, but she wasn't telling him that—or explaining that she'd had precious little sleep while he'd been away.

'Too much wine with lunch,' she dismissed, sitting up slowly, smiling as she remembered how relaxed that pleasant meal had been, how naturally they'd been able to talk together, to laugh. They might have been two totally different people. It could have ended differently, of course, she recollected. Because while they'd been waiting for their lamb cutlets to arrive, and they'd broached their first bottle of wine, she'd decided to attack rather than wait for him to chew over their marriage—as he'd threatened. So she'd asked, 'See much of Edwina these days?' and he'd looked puzzled for a moment, as if he couldn't remember who in the world Edwina was. Then he'd questioned, 'Why bring her up? That's twice you've mentioned her—as far as I recall you only met her a couple of times.' Which had told her exactly nothing.

But after that Leon had led the conversation along other, less contentious paths and, unsurprised, she had found herself thoroughly enjoying his company, happily agreeing to his suggestion that they walk to the lake to help them digest the delicious but enormous helping of home-made apricot tart and cream they'd finished up with.

Not wanting to question his present lack of interest in the 'serious talk' he had seemed so anxious to have, she had set out to enjoy herself. And, thinking about it, since her revelations in the car he hadn't once mentioned the troubled subject of their marriage, and that was fine by her, because she wanted to go on taking pleasure from the day, from his uncomplicated mood. The outing would soon be over, and another week or two would see her moving out of his life forever.

Something sharp, remarkably like sadness, wrenched at her heart. It threw out implications she didn't want to contemplate, so she clambered to her feet, clutching the rug, gabbling, 'I fell asleep almost as soon as we got here—you can blame it on all the sun, fresh air and wine—but you must have been bored out of your head.'

'Not at all,' he denied, taking the rug from her and bunching it up under one arm. 'I've been sitting here, watching you, and thinking. I've had time to sort things out in my mind.'

'Oh.' There was no answer to that. Whatever his thoughts had been during the long hot afternoon, she didn't want to know them. They wouldn't make comfortable hearing, she was sure of that. Not looking at him, she straightened her rumpled skirt, brushing away a few clinging wisps of grass. 'Time to get back, I suppose.'

'Mmm. It's gone half-past nine.' He sounded abstracted, and he seemed deep in thought as he led the way over the grassy bank, finding the footpath that traversed the wood they had wandered through on their walk quite easily.

It was dim and much cooler beneath the trees, and the birds that had poured out their liquid songs under the heavy, echoing eaves of the wood that afternoon had gone to roost, leaving the place silent—save for the occasional snapping of twigs beneath their feet. The strangely relaxing, companionable day was over, and would probably never be repeated. Fliss shivered.

'Cold?' They had been ambling slowly, and he stopped altogether now, facing her. She couldn't tell him that the shudder had come from deep inside her, an instinctive repudiation of the fact that they would never again share a day like today. In these last few hours she had been seeing a different side of him—a relaxed, unguarded side. He had treated her as a valued friend, joked with her, made her laugh, sat by her as she'd slept the afternoon away, cared about her enough to cover her gently with the rug. Tenderness was something she'd never equated with him before.

'A little.' She lifted one shoulder, answering his question, and he nodded.

'I've been thinking——' he put an arm around her shoulders, drawing her body close to his side as they began walking slowly along the track again '—it's going to take half an hour at least to get back to the car, and we'll both need a sandwich and tea, at least, before driving back to town. So it could be gone one in the morning before we make it back home.'

Fliss nodded lazily. That sounded about right. But her thoughts weren't on the possible time it might take them to get back to the apartment. Her head drooped sideways, nestling in the hollow of his shoulder. It was amazing how well their bodies fitted together, how warm and secure she felt snuggled into his side, how evenly their steps were matched—slow and measured, thigh to thigh.

As her head drooped, he splayed his fingers against the naked flesh of her upper arm, drawing her even closer to his warmth, and she made a small, involuntary cooing sound of pleasure just before he added lightly, 'Why don't we ask if they can put us up overnight at the inn? Make a really relaxed day of it, and travel back in the morning?'

'Why not?' she murmured, and felt his arm tighten around her, his head drop so that his cheek was resting against the top of her glossy head.

It was dark when they climbed the stile that led from the wood to the small car park, and as Leon helped her over she deliberately avoided his eyes. Suddenly, absurdly, she felt shy. Her agreement to his suggestion had been immediate and instinctive, but, she excused herself, it made sense. Why spoil what had turned out to be a relaxing, enjoyable day by driving back to London in the early hours when it wasn't necessary? And nothing had changed. After all, they occupied adjacent bedrooms in the apartment, and that didn't worry her. Nevertheless, she still couldn't meet his eyes, and they were still primly downcast when he left her in the small, deserted reception area while he went through to the bar to find the landlord.

'It's all fixed.' He came back moments later. 'Mrs Turner will bring sandwiches up in about ten minutes.'

As if in a dream, Fliss walked slowly to his side and he turned, smiling, as the stout, grey-haired woman who had served them with the delicious home-cooked lunch came out of the door that led to the bar, closing it on the sound of a noisy darts match in progress.

'Straight up the stairs, and it's facing you,' she instructed, smiling at Fliss who, despite her long sleep, was swaying on her feet from the fresh air and tiredness. 'I'll bring the sandwiches directly—Joe's fetching the wine from the cellar now.'

Fliss nodded, smiling sleepily, and, following Leon up the narrow, Turkey-red carpeted stairs, she wondered if she would stay awake long enough to do justice to her supper. A hot bath to wash away the stickiness of the day, a comfortable bed, and she'd be out like a light.

The corridor at the head of the stairs was dimly lit and shorter than she'd expected, and she cannoned into him as he stopped to insert a key into a heavy oak door.

'Sorry!' she gasped, her breath coming out in a whoosh as he caught her easily, an arm around her, strong fingers splayed out against the full curve of her hip.

'Any time!' He grinned softly, and she felt a slow burn of sensation cover her body because, although she was no longer off balance, he still supported her, his hand moving slowly now, like a caress, against her hip.

She began to pull away from him, not wanting to make an issue of it because today she had managed to look on him as a companion, a friend, the sexual awareness carefully battened down. She knew that if she had allowed herself to recognise the sexual power he had over her, then the easiness of the day would have been disrupted, and their time together would have degenerated into yet another sniping match. And she hadn't wanted that; she didn't want it now. This one day had to end well—it wasn't too much to ask, surely it wasn't?

As if unaware of her slight but definite withdrawal, he pushed open the door and ushered her inside, flicking on the main light to reveal a small but scrupulously clean room, a large Victorian double bed taking pride of place.

'Lovely—nice and homey,' Fliss said, moving away from him, her feet sinking into the deep pink carpet. The wallpaper was sprigged with pink and cream roses, and the furniture was all old, dark wood. The bed, with its pretty patchwork quilt, looked comfortable, and she said, her full lips curving in a smile of appreciation, 'If somebody gave me a toothbrush, I'd believe I was in heaven!'

'That's taken care of.' Leon came into the room, closing the door behind him. 'I explained the situation—no luggage—and Mrs Turner said there's no problem.' He walked over to the casement window and opened it, admitting a welcome stream of night-scented country air. 'I suspect she's geared up to meet all contingencies. They probably get their share of couples who arrive out of the blue, minus luggage. Joe was probably surprised that I didn't sign us in as Mr and Mrs Smith!'

The implications of what he had said struck Fliss hard, and her face flamed. She didn't like to imagine the motherly Mrs Turner thinking she and Leon were furtive lovers, when nothing could be further from the truth!

'It's entirely your own fault,' Leon remarked. 'If you'd kept your rings on your fingers instead of hurling them back at me, then the Turners wouldn't have an excuse for leaping to wrong conclusions!'

She had to admit he was right, but there'd been an edge to his voice she didn't like. But she wouldn't let today end by fighting him, by hurling recriminations. She would *not*! So she simply shrugged, forcing a smile, fibbing, 'It really doesn't worry me. Now—shall we see if your room's as comfortable as mine?'

But a firm knock on the door heralded the arrival of the landlord's wife with a heavily laden tray, and Leon stepped forward immediately, taking it from her and putting it down on a low, carved blanket-chest which was flanked by two chintz-covered armchairs. 'Thank you, Mrs Turner. It all looks very good.'

'It's a pleasure.' Bright brown eyes twinkled in the wrinkled face, and Fliss cringed inside, wondering what was going on inside that head! But she found some consolation when she reminded herself that Mrs Turner would discover that both rooms had been used, both beds slept in, when she went to ready the rooms for the next occupants.

'Do you have everything you need?' Mrs Turner enquired. 'If there's anything else, just give me a shout.'

'Fliss?' Leon dipped his head towards the laden tray, and she automatically flicked her eyes over it, noting the crusty bread beef sandwiches, the salad, wine. There was also a tube of toothpaste and two toothbrushes in cellophane wrappers.

'I can't think of anything else.' She smiled at the other woman and felt her eyes slide away as that lady answered with a knowing little grin.

'Then I'll leave you two in peace. Have a good night.'

'You're actually blushing,' Leon remarked slowly, as if he couldn't quite believe his eyes, and the heat in Fliss's face intensified, much to her annoyance.

'Silly, isn't it?' she managed thickly. She couldn't blame him for that slight, disbelieving frown. He wouldn't have expected this display of modesty—not after she'd told him she'd had dozens of lovers!

'We *are* married,' Leon told her tersely, and Fliss brushed that reminder aside quickly.

'But she obviously believes otherwise,' she said, and coloured even more furiously when the thought occurred that unused beds could be convincingly rumpled, and that Mrs Turner would be wise to that horny old ruse!

But it didn't really matter what others thought, did it? she consoled herself, her eyes sliding away from Leon's sardonically amused scrutiny. She knew that she wouldn't be sharing Leon's bed tonight—or any other night—and that was all that counted. That the hypothetical thought of sharing his bed actually sent a curling lick of white-hot sensation through her loins was something she didn't want to consider. So she said brightly, changing the charged subject, 'Those sandwiches look delicious, I'm starving again.' She marched over to one of the armchairs and flopped down, the full skirts of her sun-dress billowing around her long, shapely legs. While she loaded a plate from the tempting food on the tray, Leon followed more slowly, pouring red wine into the two glasses provided before sitting down.

Unaccountably, Fliss felt nervous. The palms of her hands were clammy, the pulse in her long, exposed throat beating rapidly. There was a change in Leon which she couldn't identify. He was no longer the arrogant swine—telling her what to do, and when, and why—of the past weeks. Neither was he the easy companion she had found today. She didn't quite know what he was; he seemed a stranger. She didn't know how to react to the man who was watching her silently across the supper-tray. She didn't know how to cope.

Without thinking, she lifted her wine-glass and drained the contents recklessly, aware of his eyes on her all the time. Silvery eyes, the pupils intensely black. She picked up a sandwich, although she no longer felt hungry, her fingers nervous. Suddenly and belatedly she wished she hadn't worn this particular sun-dress; the deeply scooped neckline, the tight-fitting bodice that moulded her generous breasts like a second skin, left very little to the imagination. Horrified with herself, she felt her breasts harden, the aroused nipples pushing against the fine cotton fabric, defying the flimsy barrier.

'As soon as we've eaten, we'll take a look at your room, shall we?' she mumbled around a mouthful of bread and beef. 'I don't know about you, but I'm ready for bed.'

She almost choked when he replied, with pointed significance, 'This is my room, and, believe me, I'm just as ready for bed as you.'

'Oh. Well——' She gulped, trying to control the tremor of nerves that produced a wobble in her voice, standing up hurriedly, dropping her half-eaten sandwich back on her plate. 'If you tell me where to find my room, I'll toddle along.'

She was behaving like a nervous spinster of uncertain years, and she despised herself for it. Where was the self-possessed, cool young woman she had fashioned with such care over the past four years? Gone, she acknowledged with silent anguish. Gone and almost forgotten before the alarming, very potent sexuality of this man who was, frighteningly, a stranger to her.

He was on his feet now, straddle-legged, his thumbs hooked into the low-slung waistband of his snug-fitting black denims, casual, relaxed, yet watchful. Always watchful.

Fliss moistened dry lips, tried to force a smile, told herself to hold out a hand for her room key, but could do neither of these things. She simply stared, wide-eyed, as he told her lightly, 'This is your room. My room,' and, as if needing to hammer the point home, 'Our room.'

She should have known! Hadn't she known, for four long years, just what a devious swine he was? The reality of the situation struck her starkly. He had repeatedly said that he wanted to talk about their marriage—probably to try to persuade her to be a more willing and docile partner in his hateful scheme to use her to frighten away those of his women who had the temerity to want a more permanent position in his life. He had practically kidnapped her in order to do so! But on the way here he had changed his mind. She had given him ample evidence of how easily he could affect her physically, so he had set out to be an affectionate companion, lulling her into a false sense of security. So much so that she had been more than willing to agree to spend the night here!

Had he reasoned that he could use his body to persuade her to accept the intolerable situation more successfully than a million words?

Today had all been a farce, play-acting, part of yet another of his devious schemes. And she lashed out at him before the regret could bite more deeply.

'So you didn't see fit to ask for two rooms?' She was already on her way to the door. 'I'll see to it right now.'

Then he told her calmly, his voice stopping her dead in her tracks, 'They don't have two rooms. At least, not for letting. This is a very small inn, and this is the only guest-room they have on offer.' Then, with careful lack of emphasis, he pointed out, 'Today was good. I felt for the first time ever that you and I were friends. Don't spoil it by throwing a childish tantrum.'

Childish tantrum? He didn't know what he was talking about! 'And what am I supposed to do?' she enquired acidly. 'Climb into bed with you, forget the past, welcome you with eager arms?'

He ignored her biting sarcasm, telling her wearily, 'I won't touch you, if that's what you're worrying about. But it would be a good idea to forget the damned past, build on what we discovered in each other today.' He dragged his fingers through his midnight hair, leaving it rumpled. 'You know I want a true reconciliation.'

'And we both know why!' she snapped, ignoring the tug at her heart which his suddenly vulnerable appearance provoked. 'To keep your mistresses at a safe distance! You've already used me to that end—I know exactly why you took me to that restaurant, complete with the rings you'd so thoughtfully provided!' she snorted, anger making her careless of what she said, of what she might reveal. 'I almost believed you cared something for me—believed it right up to the time you introduced me to that woman. I saw the look in your eyes, and I saw the look in hers! You couldn't contain your glee, and she—well, I know pain when I see it!'

She was burning with rage, her eyes glittering with it, her breath coming in shallow, aching gasps. Whatever he did, whatever he said, he had an ulterior motive, and one thing she was sure of—he would never use her again. Never!

'Is that what you think?' he asked levelly. 'You're far from right, you know.'

She ignored that. She wouldn't listen to his barefaced lies. 'You can sleep on one of the chairs!' She marched over to the bed and pulled off the quilt, hurling it on to the chair he'd been using earlier. 'Now you can take a walk while I get undressed,' she grated, adding venomously, 'Is there a bathroom in this damned place?'

'Through there.' He tipped his head in the direction of a narrow door beyond the bed, telling her suavely, 'Your father and stepmother may not have known how to deal with your tantrums, but you don't fool me, Fliss.'

And what did the devil mean by that snide remark? she fumed, glaring at the door he had just closed behind him as if it, and it alone, were responsible for all her present miseries. And she hadn't expected him to meekly do as she'd directed; it wasn't in character.

All at once the anger left her, left her feeling deflated and empty. Dragging her eyes from the door he had closed behind him, she turned to the bathroom. Take a walk, she'd said, and he'd done just that. But if she didn't get a move on he could well be back before she was decently tucked up in bed with the light out.

The bathroom was tiny, built into the shape of the roof, its dormer window curtained in a dark green to match the porcelain fitments. She showered and brushed her teeth in record time, and, aware that Leon could be returning at any moment, rinsed out her panties and bra very sketchily and draped them over the towel-rail to dry.

Scuttling back to the bedroom, completely naked, she hung the crumpled yellow sun-dress in the wardrobe, doused the light, then leapt into bed, pulling the covers up to her eyes.

She lay for what seemed like hours, misery gnawing at her heart, and the moon rose, slipping its beams through the open window, tracing its silvery path across the room. Her ears were aching from the strain of listening for a sound that might alert her to his return, and she began to cry—bitter tears, harsh sobs that shook her body. He was not coming back. She had told him to go, and he had gone. Where? Had he driven back to London? Would he send Spike with the car to pick her up in the morning—an unwanted piece of baggage? But that would be preferable to spending the night together in the same room, wouldn't it? She didn't know. She didn't know anything any more. Her emotions were confused, her thoughts going round her mind like mice on a treadmill.

'Fliss?' There was a wealth of concern in the voice that finally alerted her to his presence. She hadn't heard him enter the room. 'Fliss.' A hand on her head, gentle fingers sliding through the spread of her rumpled hair. A sob solidified in her chest, burning her, and she slowly turned her head on the soft white pillow to see his face on a level with hers.

He had hunkered down, and the moonlight softened the harsh planes of his face, wiping away the cynical arrogance, leaving only pure male beauty.

'Don't cry.' His voice was a whisper, his hand a caress as he wiped the tears from her face. His touch was gentle, like the slow, cool drift of silk against her heated skin, and he would make love to her, she could see it in his eyes. She wanted to cry all over again, because he hadn't left her, because he was here. And close.

'I can't bear to see you cry,' he murmured huskily. 'I won't let anything hurt you, ever again.' He held her brimming eyes with his, a promise there if she wanted to read it, and she longed to throw her arms around him and beg him to love her, because the lack of his love was the only thing that could hurt her. And then she knew the truth—he would make love to her, the intent was there in his moon-silvered eyes, and nothing she could do would prevent it—her weak female body would see to that. And then what? More heart-break? She didn't know, but suddenly, as his fingers trailed the length of her throat, finding the tiny, tell-tale pulsebeat, it didn't matter. Nothing mattered, nothing existed outside the confines of this moon-patterned room where a man called to his woman in the primitive, powerful language of unspoken need.

Slowly, as if there were all the time in the world, he eased back the covers, exposing her naked body to the moon—and his eyes. The mattress dipped as he sat on the edge of the bed, his eyes trailing a path of electric sensation over the length of her body.

'You are the most beautiful thing I have ever seen,' he told her hoarsely, his hands following the path his eyes had so recently taken, sliding over her shoulders to cup her breasts, and on over her ribcage to the satin softness of her belly, her thighs. And she could not have stopped him, not even if her life had depended on it, because from the first moment he had touched her everything else was forgotten.

She had known for some time that her physical attraction to him was more intense than it had been when she was eighteen. She hadn't been able to understand it because she was older now, wiser, more sophisticated. But she understood it now. There had been, and never would be, any other man for her.

'When we were first married, you believed you weren't capable of earning love from anyone. I want to show you just how lovable you are.' His voice was unsteady. 'But there's all the time we need.' He bent his head and kissed her breasts, and she was engulfed in flame. 'I want to show you how good it can be for us; I want to wipe out the past.'

She couldn't speak, and watched, mesmerised, as he removed his own clothes and lay down beside her, pulling her into his arms, skin searing skin until she could have cried out with the beauty of the sensations that were taking her over, filling her.

Slowly, his mouth took possession of hers, the gentle movement of his lips, his tongue, more erotic than anything she could have dreamed possible.

He whispered against her lips, 'Touch me.'

Shyly, she began stroking him, from his hair-roughened chest to the flat planes of his stomach, the lean arch of his pelvis, and a low growl of male pleasure rippled his throat as he deepened the kiss, drawing her soul into his as surely as he drew the soft contours of her lush female body to the demanding, dominant hardness of his.

Beneath her hands his flesh burned with heat, and she began to explore all of him in a way she had never dared when they'd first been married. Then, she had lain beside him, stiff with nervous tension, unable to give or to receive. But the barriers were down now, and she knew herself for what she was—a deeply sensual woman, worthy of loving, capable of giving, and she arched her hips to his in sensuous invitation, gasping with a pleasure so overwhelming that she thought she might die of it when he entered her. As he penetrated her a hoarse cry was torn from him, and she wrapped her arms around him, loving him, moving instinctively with him.

'Tell me you've ached for me as much as I've ached for you,' he pleaded huskily as she matched the slow, lingering thrusts of his body. 'Tell me.'

She groaned, incapable of speech, her mouth open against his skin, tasting his sweat, tasting the tremors of desire that rippled through his nerve-ends, his very heartbeat. And she knew, as he transported her to a beauty she had never known before, that she loved him. She had always loved him. And she knew that the love she was capable of giving now was fuller, richer by far, and more enduring than the love he had awoken in that earlier, younger, insecure self.

She awoke in the quiet grey hour before dawn, slipping silently out of bed. She didn't want to wake him. She needed a little time, just a little time, to adjust to what she knew about herself.

Their lovemaking had transcended anything she had ever dreamed possible as time and again he had taken them both to the very heights of ecstasy. And just before he had fallen asleep in her arms he had murmured, 'We're going to have a true marriage, Fliss. You're mine, only mine. The past doesn't exist.'

And whether he meant his past or hers—with her supposed string of lovers—she didn't know. Hers, she supposed wryly, her eyes limpid with love as she glanced back at his sprawled male body, deep in sleep.

She had matured ten years in the last few hours, and, although she knew that a leopard couldn't change its spots any more than Leon Draker could change the womanising habits of a lifetime, she could accept it—just. To deny her abiding love for him now would be like cutting herself in half.

The early-morning air drifting through the open window was chilly, making her shiver, and she wrapped herself in the quilt she'd angrily tossed on the chair the night before and huddled into its welcoming folds.

She could see her future quite clearly, an echo of the past, yet different—the empty rooms, the silent telephone, long hours when she would lie awake wondering where he was. But this time she wouldn't let it get to her in the same way, she would cope, because her love for him was cataclysmic, her earlier, puny efforts to control it as effective as trying to plug an erupting volcano with a child's balloon.

And so she would stay with him, always, loving him, always, taking what he had to offer because it was good. No longer did she care that he knew how his slightest touch could set her alight. He could murder her pride, but he couldn't murder love.

Smiling a little, she stared from the window, quietly amazed by her own total acceptance, the maturity that had given her the strength to acknowledge her love, to stay with him. There would be agony ahead for her, she knew that. But there would also be joy. The joy of giving love, giving it whole-heartedly, without making demands.

Slowly, the morning came to brightness, the sky spreading fingers of light over the land, the mist hanging heavily in the dips between the hills, shimmering with the opalescent colours of dawn.

Fliss dropped her hands, letting the quilt fall to the floor, and padded on soft, naked feet back to the bed where her husband was stirring, reaching out for her.

## CHAPTER TEN

'I'M going to arrange a holiday—a long one. How does the idea of the Bahamas grab you?' He was knotting his tie, his eyes soft, and Fliss stood up on tiptoe to put a kiss on the end of his nose, her own eyes drowsy.

'Sounds heavenly.'

She wasn't wearing anything at all, except a turban-tied towel around her hair, and she could feel the tremors of need that shook the hard male body beneath the civilised trappings of formal business gear. And she felt powerful, all woman, delighting in her new-found sensuality, in her love for him.

'Fliss——' His voice was low, rough. Managing the simple task of mastering his tie seemed beyond him, and she moved away reluctantly, finding a robe and slipping into it, her voice warm with husky laughter as she sympathised.

'I know! But you have work to do—and that holiday to arrange—and we've already spent longer in the shower than was decent! But I'll see you later—how much later?'

She kept her voice light. She wasn't trying to tie him down. If their marriage was to work, she must never do that. He promised, 'No later than I need be. I should be finished by mid-afternoon.'

She nodded, moving to the dressing-table, unwinding the towel from her hair. It had been almost eleven by the time they'd arrived back in London, and there had been genuine regret in Leon's voice as he'd told her, 'I'm afraid I have to put in a few hours today. But I need a shower first. Join me?'

'I feel tacky, too,' she'd said, plucking at the crumpled yellow sun-dress. But the lilt in her heart had confirmed that cleanliness was not her first reason for accepting his invitation, and he'd grinned then, delighted with her, and the shower had lasted more than an hour.

Now, he came to stand behind her, reflected grey eyes holding sapphire, and he said huskily, 'I shall never be able to tell you how much last night meant to me.' His hands rested gently on her hips, and she could feel the pressure of each firm finger pad through the thin fabric of her robe. 'We finally buried the past—you'll let it stay that way, Fliss?' Suddenly, the face that watched her through the mirror was drawn, his voice holding a raw anguish as he asserted thickly, 'You're my wife. Don't ever forget it again.'

His hands moved upwards, the warm vibrancy of his touch sending ecstatic shudders through her as he grasped her shoulders and hauled her round to face him, his eyes dark with nameless emotion.

And Fliss said raggedly, her heart flipping over because he was asking her to forget Edwina and all the others in between—and to overlook the unknown procession of his future affairs, 'How could I forget I'm your wife? I don't suppose you'd let me if I wanted to!'

'Too right.' A wry smile teased one corner of his wide, chiselled mouth, and his eyes lightened, admitting the silvery lights of laughter that had the power to make her weak with love for him. 'And here's something to ensure you remember. I want you to wear them—and not for the crazy reason you dreamt up—but that's something we're going to have to thrash out later.'

He took the rings from an inner pocket, holding her hand with one of his while he pushed them in place, and she was still looking at them long after he'd closed the bedroom door behind him on his way out. They were going to have to thrash it out, he'd said. She wasn't sure if she wanted to hear all about his troublesome mistresses!

The large sapphire felt heavy, the beautiful stone, the golden bands a weight she couldn't ignore. His marks of ownership. There was no doubt he wanted her on two counts—as a woman and as a wife. His desire for her couldn't have been faked, and for as long as that lasted he would find pleasure in her bed. Hers alone? She couldn't be sure, but she knew that when desire palled, as no doubt it would, her role as his wife would, as the shield he would hide behind when conducting his discreet affairs, come into play. He seemed congenitally incapable of remaining faithful to one woman. Had Edwina done that to him? Soured him? Had she refused to marry him, tie herself down, even after Fliss had walked out all that time ago? Was that one of the reasons Leon hadn't insisted on divorce? She didn't know, and doubted if she would ever discover the truth.

Recognising the onset of one of the first dark moods of introspection—moods that would colour the rest of her life, if she let them—she made a robust effort to talk some sense into herself as she dressed quickly in a cream silk-and-wool-mix skirt and a black silk shirt blouse. She had accepted his lovemaking, her position as his wife in every sense of the word, with her eyes wide open. And maybe, she thought with inculcated optimism as she brushed her long, unmanageable mane of raven hair and stepped into elegant, classic black shoes, if she could always be truly generous with her very real love for him, he might cease to wander, stop looking elsewhere for excitement, begin to love her just a little.

Still in a determinedly optimistic mood, she headed for the kitchen. Spike was loading the washing machine and Fliss said, 'Hi, there!' totally unprepared for his frosty reply.

'There have been three telephone calls for you, madam—all from the same gentleman. A Mr Harlie. I told him that you and your husband had been detained, but he insisted on leaving a message. I didn't like to mention this while Mr Draker was here.'

He slammed the door of the machine home and straightened up, and Fliss, unable to understand his reversion to his former, disapproving attitude, asked, 'What was the message?'

'That you should meet him at one o'clock today at the Green Street restaurant. He said you'd know which one he meant.' He released his words as if he were parting with teeth, and Fliss understood what it was all about now. Of course! Spike thought the caller was one of the string of lovers Annabel Draker had spoken of! He thought she was well on the way to breaking his beloved master's heart all over again. If only he knew! It was funny, in a sick way.

'It's all right, Spike,' she said gently, resisting the impulse to pat him on top of his balding head—thus ruining his precious dignity forever. 'There's not a single thing to worry about.'

She had grown fond of the tiny man. He was fiercely partisan and comically pedantic, a character in his own right, and she bestowed a wide and unanswered smile on him and left the kitchen to fetch the jacket that went with the skirt she was wearing, wondering why Gerald was in town and so obviously anxious to see her. It had to have something to do with the merger.

The restaurant in Green Street was small, intimate and hair-raisingly expensive. At Netta's insistence, the three of them had spent a weekend break in London a couple of years ago. It had been a hectic, happy time for all of them, and the high spot had been dinner in this very place. It had been Fliss's birthday, and the lavish meal had been their gift to her. It had been an evening to remember, an extravagance that had touched her deeply.

'I'm glad you could make it. I was beginning to think I'd miss you. I have to catch an afternoon train back,' Gerald told her over their dry martinis. 'It was like getting blood out of a stone, trying to prise information out of whoever it was who answered your phone.'

'Spike,' Fliss explained absently, her eyes taking in every detail of her former boss's appearance. He didn't look like a man whose firm was about to go bankrupt, she decided. He looked fitter and more relaxed than she'd seen him look since Netta's death. So the merger had to be going well.

'Any news of the merger?' she asked, keeping her voice light, twisting the stem of her glass, not quite able to hide the slight tension. And Gerald smiled easily, leaning back as a soft-footed waiter placed their moules marinière in front of them.

'It's all tied up, love. Didn't Leon tell you? He and his company solicitor spent a couple of days with us last week. It's in the bag!' He grinned widely.

So that accounted for his air of genial relaxation, Fliss thought, and it certainly accounted for the brilliant smile she gave him as she picked up her fork. Leon hadn't gone back on his word. She should have known that he kept his word where business was concerned.

But her smile faded when Gerald said seriously, 'Is everything all right with you, Fliss?'

'Fine,' she answered stoically. 'Couldn't be better,' adding to herself, I've just tied myself for life to a man I love. A man who lusts after me, but doesn't love me. A man with a roving eye and feet to match! Why shouldn't I be fine?

But Gerald, apparently, wasn't satisfied with that. Toying with his food, frowning over it, he persisted, 'I expected Leon would have brought you with him to Marton Clee. You could both have stayed at the Grange. He must know how close we are.'

'Sure he does,' Fliss dismissed airily, not adding that, as far as Leon was concerned, Gerald had been one of her lovers! The last place Leon would have taken her to was Gerald's home. 'I was tied up,' she prevaricated, feeling like a louse. 'We're taking an extended holiday—the Bahamas, I think,' she added as if that excused everything. 'You can imagine the amount of shopping I have to do.'

He seemed satisfied with that, genuinely relieved that this second attempt at marriage was working out, and Fliss made a firm mental note to tell Leon the truth. He mustn't be allowed to continue to think of Gerald as one of her many ex-lovers. Not if they were to be close business colleagues. And perhaps it was time for her to come clean, to tell Leon that, far from the 'dozens' she had taunted him with, there had been no one in all of those four lonely years.

Poor Gerald! She looked at him fondly. He would be horrified to learn that she had allowed Leon to continue in his mistaken assessment of their relationship. Horrified and painfully embarrassed. It would seem like incest! She was ashamed of herself for allowing the deception to continue for as long as it had.

As the meal progressed at a leisurely pace, Gerald seemed to grow more withdrawn, his eyes rarely meeting hers now, his conversational efforts just that. His initial and unfeigned pleasure at seeing her again had given way to an almost morose unease. Declining the dessert menu, Fliss asked, 'What's wrong, Gerald?' Shaking her head as he produced an obviously simulated look of surprise, a disclaimer that anything at all could be wrong, she added, 'You invite me to lunch at one of the most expensive restaurants in town, then sit there looking as though you wished yourself a million miles away.'

His face was dull red. 'I don't know how to tell you this,' his eyes slid away from hers, 'but I want you to be the first to know. That's important to me.'

'Know what?' she prompted, her eyes darkening, puzzled.

But he replied evasively, 'Remember the time when Netta and I brought you here?'

'And we'd been to Hampton Court and got caught in the rain,' she supplied, doing her best to look patient.

'And it was your birthday—and Netta had too much champagne and couldn't stop giggling on the way back to the hotel in the taxi . . .'

They smiled at the shared memories, at each other, then Fliss said firmly, 'Gerald—just what is wrong?'

It came out in a rush, his voice low and quick, 'I'm getting married again. It may not be the romance of the century, but we're very fond of each other, have tastes and attitudes in common. And we're both lonely. It's Amy—Amy Prentiss.'

His secretary! For a moment, Fliss could only gape. Amy had been with Gerald for fifteen years, a pleasant uncomplicated woman, who had never married because her invalid mother had relied on her. And if Fliss had been asked to map Gerald's future, she couldn't have wished for anything better for him.

'I know you loved Netta—you looked on her as a mother,' Gerald mumbled. 'You probably think I'm callous——'

'I think nothing of the sort!' Fliss denied roundly. 'I know there'll never be another Netta for you, but you and Amy will make each other very happy. Netta would have been the last person to want to see you pining and lonely for the rest of your life.' She reached out to place her hand reassuringly over his. Marriage to Amy would be the best thing that could happen for both of them, and she said so, willing the light to return to his eyes. It did, and his other hand came over hers, trapping it between both of his and he smiled.

'I was afraid you wouldn't understand——'

From somewhere an icily smooth voice cut in, 'Spike told me I might still find you here.'

'Won't you join us?' Gerald was already on his feet, relinquishing Fliss's hand reluctantly.

Leon said, 'I'm afraid I've come to tear my wife away,' his tone perfectly polite, but chilling.

'Of course—Fliss was telling me you are about to take off for the Bahamas. I envy you.' Gerald was fussing like an old hen—something he always did when he felt out of his depth—and Fliss thought she understood the reason for Leon's frigid manner. Now was as good a time as any to put him right over his wrong assumption about her relationship with Gerald. Telling him of Gerald's wedding plans would do for openers.

Forcing an insouciant smile, she looked up into her husband's shuttered face, about to tell him Gerald's news, and heard him say drily, in response to Gerald's remark, 'I'm sure you do, Harlie. I'm damned sure you do.'

'Leon——' Fliss reached out to put a pacifying hand on his arm. The fine, mid-grey fabric felt cold to her touch, as if no one inhabited the immaculate suit of clothing.

'Later,' he said tightly, taking her arm and hauling her from her seat in a gesture that might have looked chivalrous to an outsider, but felt like a threat.

'Sorry to have spoiled the party, Harlie.' He was already steering Fliss towards the door, and she looked up at him, forgetting Gerald. Leon's eyes were black, black and cold and fathomless, his mouth a grim slash in a face that was otherwise devoid of expression.

As soon as she had realised he had tracked her to the restaurant, she had experienced the first *frisson* of unease. That he would put the wrong interpretation on the scene was a foregone conclusion. But she wished he had been easier on Gerald—he would be wondering what the hell was going on! However, Leon would understand when he heard the truth.

Outside, on the sun-warmed pavement, he dropped her arm, moving away as if her nearness disgusted him. She had expected his anger, but not that it would take this form: cold, distant, divorced from normal heated reaction.

'It isn't what you think it is,' she said quickly.

He replied disinterestedly, 'I'm afraid I don't believe you. It's exactly what I think—that you couldn't wait to meet him again, that you had to tell him you might be away for some time—wifely duties in the Bahamas—what a bore! There's a cab waiting for you,' he indicated the black vehicle a few yards away, its engine idling, the driver looking half asleep. 'Go back to the apartment and pack. I want you out by the time I get there this evening. I never want to see you again. My solicitor will contact yours about the divorce.'

## CHAPTER ELEVEN

SHE would leave, but not without telling him exactly what she thought of him, Fliss vowed, her mouth grim.

After the initial shock had worn off, she had packed haphazardly, and the suitcases were in her bedroom, her rings on the dressing-table, and she was in the lounge doggedly sitting it out.

How dared he treat her that way? she fumed. How dared he? She wasn't something he'd bought on approval and decided to return, dissatisfied—as if she were shoddy goods! She was his wife, dammit, and she deserved better—especially as it had been he who had insisted she go back to him!

She jerked up off the chair she'd been perching on, and started to pace the floor. So, OK, he'd walked in on what he'd wrongly assumed to be a lovers' meeting, but he only had himself to blame for that mistaken assumption, she justified. Besides, he had been scathing about her so-called affair with Gerald before, but that hadn't stopped him from demanding she return to him. So why this talk of divorce now? Why tip her out on the streets at this stage of the game? The man had to be demented!

Only by keeping her anger at white-hot pitch could she prevent herself from creeping ignominiously away and finding a place to hide and cry her heart out for all she had lost. He was the only man for her, that was the pity of it all, and now what slim chance she had had of finding a kind of happiness had been killed stone-dead with a few words from him.

She gave the carriage clock a fulminating glare. Would the devil never come baçk? Spike had gone to bed two hours ago, and it was well after midnight. So where was he? Consoling himself with Charlotte, or someone like her? And how did he think he was going to be able to fob the other woman off in the future? When Charlotte heard of the divorce there would be no holding her back! But maybe he thought it worth any amount of future hassle, just as long as he would be rid of a wife he could no longer tolerate. Maybe their lovemaking hadn't given him the satisfaction which she, in her idiocy, had imagined it had. Fliss had no experience whatsoever to guide her in that department.

Not liking the paths her thoughts were taking her down, she began to head for the kitchen and the coffee-pot when a muted whine told her that someone was using the lift. He had decided to come home.

Her heart began to pump erratically, and her feet were rooted to the spot, her hands clammy. She didn't know how she was going to face him and not let her love for him show. But he would be angry because she was still here, and she was angry, too, and rage could hide a multitude of other emotions. So when he stepped out of the lift, she was ready for him.

He looked weary, she thought, his face strained. But it was only a second before the icy, indifferent mask was in place.

'I asked you to go,' he stated unemotionally.

Matching his tone, she said, 'I know you did. But I don't creep out with my tail between my legs—it's not my style.'

He ignored that, walking further into the room, sparing a glance for his wrist-watch.

'I meant it,' he told her coldly. 'I want you out of here. It's late, but if you phone around you'll find a hotel to take you in.'

Calmly, with dignity, she walked to one of the sofas and sat down. She would leave, she wouldn't stay where she was so obviously not wanted, but first she said, 'I have no intention of going anywhere until I've said what I have to say. After that, you won't see me for dust.'

'Cut the wounded act.' He gave her an exasperated look. 'We made a bargain, you and I—or so I thought. We were making a second attempt, and you promised to stay away from Gerald.'

'I did no such thing!' she yelped. Her control was already beginning to slip. She would have to take more care. Her emotions could have a field day as soon as she had found somewhere to hide. Until then it was wiser, safer, to keep her feelings firmly battened down. 'Do you make a habit of inventing things to suit yourself?' she added frigidly.

Momentarily, his eyes glittered and a flush of rage burned beneath his skin, but he replied icily enough, 'Your future faithfulness was implied. I said we had buried the past—that, as far as I was concerned, it didn't exist. You also agreed that you wouldn't "forget" you were my wife.'

Speechless, Fliss stared at him from stormy eyes, and he threw at her, 'Yet barely an hour after making love with me, you were rushing to keep an assignation with sugar-daddy. Do you honestly wonder that I couldn't stomach the thought of you sharing my life?' The anger was showing through now, and would have alarmed her had not hers been rising, too, threatening to run away with her despite all her good intentions. 'What were you doing?' his voice cracked like a whip. 'Arranging when it would be mutually convenient for him to take some anonymous hotel room to have you in?'

There was a steely hue in her sapphire eyes. 'You make me ill!' she snapped. 'It's the old double standard raising its hoary old head. You forced me to come back to you simply because you wanted to use me, and our marriage, to ward off a mistress who was becoming too dependent. And if that's not sickening enough in itself—it was OK for you to bed Edwina, eight weeks into our marriage, yet you practically foam at the mouth because you *think* I'm having an affair with Gerald!'

He had grown very still. 'What did you say?' A muscle moved convulsively at the side of his jaw.

Fliss ground her teeth. 'Do you want me to paint a picture?'

'That's the third time you've mentioned Edwina.' He threw her an angry, puzzled look. 'And why the hell should I have gone to bed with her? Eight weeks into our marriage you walked out on me. I was too busy trying to get to grips with what you'd done to take any woman to bed—let alone Edwina.'

'I'm almost crying for you!' she bit out sarcastically, controlling the urge to leap up and slap his handsome face. 'I walked out on you *because* you took Edwina to your bed!'

There, it was out, the things she'd vowed she would never say to him. But what did pride matter now? Nothing mattered now.

'Explain,' he commanded softly, dangerously. 'It's all news to me.'

Fliss eyed him doubtfully. He was still lying; he had to be. She had seen what she had seen. He would always lie to her.

'It doesn't matter,' she said, her voice drained and expressionless. She got to her feet, her legs wooden, difficult to move. What was the use in raking over the sordid past? If she produced a photograph, he would still deny the incident had happened.

'It matters.' He was in front of her, dwarfing her. He must have moved at the speed of light. 'So tell me.'

She flicked her tongue over her lips. Her face was hot, her throat tight. The scene that had remained locked in her heart for four long years was almost impossible to put into words.

'You can't have forgotten,' she said acidly. 'Or have you made love to her so many times you can't readily recall the exact occasion I'm speaking of?' she accused.

'I have never made love to Edwina in my life,' he stated harshly. 'The thought never occurred. I never even fancied her.' His long, male mouth twisted grimly. 'My mother wanted me to marry Edwina, but, as I pointed out, time after time, I would have rather married a rattlesnake.'

He spoke with such conviction that, had she not seen him in bed with Edwina, she would have believed him. But she *had* seen them together. She turned away from him angrily and walked to the other end of the room to pour herself a generous dose of brandy.

Her back still to him, she stated unequivocally, 'From the moment I set foot inside Feathergay your mother made her feelings very plain. No way was I fit to be your wife. Then Edwina came on the scene and, according to her, not only was I unfit to be your wife, but I held that exalted position only because you married me to get your revenge on her! You were in love with her, always had been——' She took a mouthful of brandy, feeling it burn her throat. 'But she had been indiscreet with some Austrian baron, and you found out. And so, instead of marrying her, as planned, you married the first totally unsuitable nothing you could find.'

She walked unsteadily to a chair and slumped down. 'I had the pretty story directly from the horse's mouth,' she explained with jerky patience. She didn't look at him, because this was something not even he could wriggle out of, and, oddly enough, she didn't want to witness his defeat.

'I was insecure enough in those days to believe almost anything,' she went on doggedly. 'That I was gauche, badly dressed, inferior in every way to the Drakers of Feathergay, I already knew. But I doubt if I would have truly believed Edwina if I hadn't gone to your room and seen you in bed together. So I walked out. And, if it's any comfort to you,' she tagged on bitterly, 'there never was a lover back home.

He was entirely a figment of your mother's imagination.'

'I can't believe I'm hearing this.' His voice was low, unsteady.

'You'd better. It's the truth,' she told him, adding sadly to herself, And you know it, but even now you won't admit it. She put her glass down, tired, suddenly so very tired.

'Explain what happened,' he said tightly. He came to sit beside her and, momentarily, something explosive burned in his eyes. 'Tell me, Fliss.'

She swallowed, weary of the whole dreadful farce, and she said gruffly, memory stirring more painfully than ever before, 'I'd been for a walk. I used to walk for hours. You were nearly always away, and your mother didn't exactly make me feel a welcome addition to the family. That day I'd been out for longer than usual. When I got back your mother was waiting for me. I couldn't think why, at first. Normally she avoided me like the plague. She told me you'd come home, that you'd asked her to tell me to go to your room. You had something to show me. I couldn't think what it could be . . .' Her voice wavered, because even now she could recall how light her heart had felt because her beloved Leon was home and wanting, at last, to share something with her. 'So I went to your room,' she continued more hardly. 'And you were in bed with Edwina, and she was naked. Even after my sorry upbringing, I had no idea that people could be so cruel. You wanted to show me how much she meant to you, and how little I did. And no matter how often you deny it, I saw what I saw—what you had meant me to see. So I left.' She looked away from him quickly, but not before she'd witnessed the black rage that burned deep in his eyes.

'I'll go now.' She stood up, her heart hurting. She would phone for a taxi, and spend what was left of the night at the station. Take the first train back to Marton Clee. Gerald would let her stay at the Grange until she could find a job and a place to live. That, at least, was something to be grateful for.

'Fliss—will you listen if I tell you what I think really happened? Every detail of that day is burned into my brain,' he added tersely, and she turned slowly, shaken by the way he looked. He looked haggard, ten years older. Unable to move, she watched from pain-filled eyes as he walked towards her.

'The day you left me, I'd left London with a clear plan of action in mind. I was going to take you away from Feathergay. I'd begun, at last, to see how out of your depth you were. You were so damned young. I had realised by then that the only chance we had together was to go away, for a time. To get to know each other without the trappings of wealth and ancestry smothering you. But driving back I developed a villainous migraine—a one-off for me. Stress, I suppose. I'd been keyed up for weeks, wondering how to save our marriage. You didn't want me near you. If I touched you, you froze.'

'I was afraid of failing you,' she defended huskily. 'You were so much older, so experienced.'

'Hell!' He looked haunted. He took her hands, and she let them lie passively in his grasp, unable to discount the sincerity of real anguish in his voice as he told her, 'To this day I'll never remember how I got the car back to Feathergay without running it into a ditch. I should have stopped to sleep off the worst of the attack, but all I could think of was getting back to you to tell you we were going to make a fresh start—away from that house. When I did get back, I asked for you. Mother told me you were out and could be some time. Edwina was there—I vaguely remember that.' He drew in a ragged breath, his grip tightening. 'Mother gave me a couple of tablets—I don't know what they were, but she suffered from migraine and took them, she said. She suggested I went upstairs to lie down, said she'd send you up as soon as you got back. The last thing I remember is falling into bed. I was out for hours. When I woke I was told that you'd walked out, gone to some other guy. And the worst part of it is that Mother must have planned it. At least, she and Edwina grasped the opportunity when it presented itself. Edwina may have been in my bed, but I wasn't aware of it. I nearly went crazy trying to figure out where I'd gone wrong with you. Then Father's death made me sober up.'

'The message she gave you wasn't the one I left,' Fliss said quietly. Knowing how Annabel had lied about that, she could at last believe Leon's version of events. Annabel had made it patently clear that she had wanted Edwina as her daughter-in-law. 'Were you engaged to Edwina?' she asked tightly.

'What do you think?' he grated. 'Mother had been throwing her at my head since the day she reached the age of sixteen! Edwina is all I dislike most in a woman—she's a selfish, shallow, beautiful bitch.' His face stiffened and he dropped her hands abruptly. 'Other people fouled our marriage up first time round, but you can't blame anyone else this time.'

'Only you.' She was trembling inside. Annabel and Edwina had set out to ruin their marriage, that was established fact. But they still had a long way to go.

'I don't see how,' he remarked, returning to the former, dismissive coldness. He poured himself a drink and tossed it back as if he needed it. 'I did every damned thing I could think of to get you back. I admit, when we were first married I was out of my depth with you. You were like a draught of clear, pure water after too much champagne, and I rushed you into marriage without giving you the chance to think it out. My instincts told me to wait, to give you time to get used to the age difference, the differences in our life-styles and backgrounds. But I was afraid of losing you. And so I rushed it, only coming to my senses when it became obvious that my passion for you both frightened and disgusted you——'

'That's not true!' she broke in, her eyes shimmering with tears. 'I was afraid you'd find me boring in bed, inexperienced and——'

'Fliss—don't!' he said roughly. 'Whatever you were then, you're a fully experienced woman now. And that's what I can't take. Not that you've had lovers,' he dismissed edgily, 'but that you refuse to remain faithful now. I said the past didn't exist, as far as I'm concerned, but the future's a different thing entirely. I can give you everything except the freedom to take lovers. I couldn't stand that.'

He put down his empty glass and faced her squarely, emotion blazing in his eyes, his face gaunt. 'Damn it all, Fliss, I love you. I've loved you since I first set eyes on you,' he said rawly.

For Fliss, the earth shook, nothing seemed solid any more. Her conceptions of this man splintered into fragments and abruptly assumed a new form. She couldn't take it in. But it was going to be all right—it had to be!

'It's all been in your mind,' she assured him shakily. Apprehensively, because she had to make him understand and she didn't know whether he was capable of it, she took a step towards him, and then another, until she was standing close, very close. She prayed he wouldn't flinch away. He didn't move. It was as if he had turned to stone. 'I've always loved you,' she admitted hoarsely. 'There have been times when I tried to tell myself I hated you—but I was lying to myself. And, loving you, there has been no other man.'

'Do you mean that?' he questioned unsteadily. 'Don't play games with me, Fliss.'

'I'm not.' She wanted to touch him, to hold him in her arms, kiss the sternness away from that mouth, banish the doubt from those eyes. In a moment, she promised herself, in just one moment...'I didn't leave you to go to a lover. I'd never had a lover, for one thing. Only you. Your mother made him up—to stop you coming after me, I suppose—to sicken you. And you assigned that role to Gerald.' She essayed a wobbly smile. They were so close. She could feel his body heat. He was scorching her, burning her up.

'I did?' His voice thickened, and he held out his hands as if to touch her, but dropped them slowly back to his sides.

She nodded, her heart knocking against her ribs. Everything depended on whether she could make him believe her. Her throat was tight, scrambling the words in her throat, but at last she managed, 'It was all in your mind. Gerald became more like a father to me than my own. Netta—well, in every way that counts Netta *was* my mother. They both took the place of my parents. Their love and understanding gave me back my confidence, made me see that I had some value.'

'And today?' He caught her chin in one hand and tipped her head back, his eyes burningly intent on hers as if he were trying to reach her soul.

There was a fierce, bright pain inside her chest, the anguished side of loving, and she told him, willing him to believe her, 'He'd been in town on business for a couple of days, and he wanted to meet me. He wanted me to be the first to know that he is planning to marry Amy, his secretary. He knew how I'd felt about Netta, and he was afraid I'd think him disloyal.'

For a timeless moment he held her eyes and she saw the doubts disappear, then he gathered her savagely into his arms, rocking her, murmuring her name against the raven sheen of her hair.

'Oh, Fliss—I thought I'd lost you this time! The first time I knew I'd get you back—even if I had to freeze hell over to do it. I had you watched, knew you were climbing the ladder at Harlie's. And from then it was only a matter of time. I engineered the situation at Harlie's with the sole intention of putting you in a position of weakness. Had I asked you to come back to me, without any leverage, you'd have laughed in my face. I staked everything on your having a social conscience. And on your feelings for Gerald. I had to have you back at any price. But today, when I discovered you were still seeing Gerald—after the rapture of our loving—I knew the price was too high to pay. Loving you has become an obsession. I would have lost my sanity—wondering who you were with, wondering how many times you'd walk away from my bed into some other guy's. I had to tell you to go—to save my sanity.'

'Don't!' she begged huskily, her throat thick with tears. She had believed him to be invincible, invulnerable. But he was only human; he had his weaknesses, like the rest. Soon, he would be as strong as ever, but now she had to be the one with strength.

She reached up, finding his lips, her tongue moving lazily, parting them. 'I love you. Only you. Always,' she murmured against his mouth. 'I love you so much—I can't begin to tell you how much.'

'Fliss——' Leon muttered thickly, his body's response coming quickly, unmistakably. He took her offered mouth, kissing her with a hunger that shook her soul. 'No one, real or imaginary, is going to come between us ever again.' He was trailing kisses down the length of her throat, burning kisses that touched her skin like wildfire, his body trembling with desire. 'Thank heaven you waited,' he said at last, scooping her into his arms.

Her body quaked with pleasure, and she twined her arms around his neck as he carried her through to her bedroom, picking his way over her suitcases. 'It would have taken more than your arrogance to send me away,' she admitted teasingly.

And later, very much later, she groaned a sleepy protest as she felt him move out of the bed. But he was back within moments, taking her hand and slipping her rings back on to her finger.

'Don't ever take them off again,' he instructed, hi voice a growly, contented purr. 'Or I'm going to hav to get them grafted on!'

'You might try!' she chuckled, opening her arm to receive his hard male body as he rejoined her be neath the covers. Then she struggled up, her hair riotous scented cloud against the piled pillows, a tin frown between her eyes.

'Did you buy those rings to impress Charlotte?' sh asked, trying to sound cross, but failing, because sh knew that whatever affairs he might have had in th past would stay in the past.

'No way,' he laughed softly, gathering her into hi arms again, his mouth making passionate foray against the warm curves of her breasts. 'You mad me so jealous when you said you'd had dozens o lovers—and would have dozens more—that I retali ated by saying the most hurtful thing I could thin of. I'd just begun to think I was getting somewher with you—you'd allowed me to hold you, to kis you—then you said you'd merely been interested t see if my technique had improved! Hell, you mad me so mad!' His lips opened, tasting and teasing on nipple until she squirmed against him, her hand sliding over the taut muscles of his back. 'I wante to hurt you—but there haven't been any mistresses Charlotte may have had ideas in that direction, I don' know. I never really saw any other woman. And I wa so proud, Fliss, to introduce you as my wife. I woul have shouted it to the whole world if I could! Now, he commanded hoarsely before his mouth plundere hers, 'no more talk.'

* * *

Leon pulled the car to a halt on the wide gravel forecourt. 'OK, darling?'

She turned loving eyes to him, seeing the tenderness reflected in the smoky grey irises, and she smiled softly. 'I'm fine. Just fine.'

His hand closed over hers reassuringly, but she didn't need reassurance—not any more. She could look at Feathergay and see it for what it was—a lovely, cherishable home.

One day she would be mistress here, and when that time came she would embrace the position gladly, with confidence. Until then, there was Annabel to deal with.

Leon slipped out of the car, his feet crunching on the gravel. He opened the door at her side, and she got out, holding the sables around her against the cold winter wind.

'Four months in the Bahamas has made me ultra-sensitive to the British winter,' she told him ruefully, and he grinned, holding her close to him for a moment before slipping an arm around her and beginning the slow walk to the house.

Above them, the wind howled high, tossing bare black branches against the grey December sky, and she wrinkled her nose. 'Let's hope Annabel has a few good fires going!'

They were spending Christmas here. Fliss had gently insisted that they accept her mother-in-law's invitation, although she knew Leon would have preferred them to be on their own—with the ever-devoted Spike in attendance. In his anger over the part his mother had played in the break-up of their marriage he had threatened to make her leave Feathergay, to cut her out of his life completely.

'She cost us four years of bitter loneliness,' he had stated. 'She lost us four years of happiness. I want nothing more to do with her—and I could put her out of her beloved Feathergay. I own the place now; Father willed it to me. She's nothing but a scheming, conniving——'

'Don't!' Fliss had stopped his bitter words with a kiss. 'She loved you, and she wanted the best for you. As far as she was concerned, Edwina was the best. People do strange things in the name of love. Besides, she loves that house. And it's all she really has now. We, my love, have each other.'

And so Annabel was to stay, and, if she could, Fliss would heal the rift—or at least patch it over so that the cracks wouldn't be too obvious. She knew she could handle anything Annabel cared to deal out—with patience and understanding, she hoped.

Looking up at the lovely house, memories stirred. Echoes of the time she had first seen it—the feelings of awe, of her own unsuitability. And meeting Annabel for the first time. Annabel had been wearing a soft cashmere dress and pearls—real pearls—and one look from those dark, cold eyes had made Fliss horribly aware of her own blatant curves, her crumpled cotton skirt and cheap sweater.

True, she still had blatant curves—and they would grow more blatant as the new baby she and Leon were so happily awaiting grew—but now they were expensively clothed in discreet elegance, and Leon's reed-slim, regal mother could intimidate her no more.

Nestling her head deeper against Leon's broad shoulder as they mounted the stone step, she smiled contentedly. Secure in Leon's love, there was nothing she could not do.

## PASSPORT TO ROMANCE VACATION SWEEPSTAKES

# OFFICIAL RULES

**SWEEPSTAKES RULES AND REGULATIONS. NO PURCHASE NECESSARY.**

**HOW TO ENTER:**

**1.** To enter, complete this official entry form and return with your invoice in the envelope provided, or print your name, address, telephone number and age on a plain piece of paper and mail to: Passport to Romance, P.O. Box #1397, Buffalo, N.Y. 14269-1397. No mechanically reproduced entries accepted.
**2.** All entries must be received by the Contest Closing Date, midnight, December 31, 1990 to be eligible.
**3.** Prizes: There will be ten (10) Grand Prizes awarded, each consisting of a choice of a trip for two people to: i) London, England (approximate retail value $5,050 U.S.); ii) England, Wales and Scotland (approximate retail value $6,400 U.S.); iii) Caribbean Cruise (approximate retail value $7,300 U.S.); iv) Hawaii (approximate retail value $ 9,550 U.S.); v) Greek Island Cruise in the Mediterranean (approximate retail value $12,250 U.S.); vi) France (approximate retail value $7,300 U.S.).
**4.** Any winner may choose to receive any trip or a cash alternative prize of $5,000.00 U.S. in lieu of the trip.
**5.** Odds of winning depend on number of entries received.
**6.** A random draw will be made by Nielsen Promotion Services, an independent judging organization on January 29, 1991, in Buffalo, N.Y., at 11:30 a.m. from all eligible entries received on or before the Contest Closing Date. Any Canadian entrants who are selected must correctly answer a time-limited, mathematical skill-testing question in order to win. Quebec residents may submit any litigation respecting the conduct and awarding of a prize in this contest to the Régie des loteries et courses du Quebec.
**7.** Full contest rules may be obtained by sending a stamped, self-addressed envelope to: "Passport to Romance Rules Request", P.O. Box 9998, Saint John, New Brunswick, E2L 4N4.
**8.** Payment of taxes other than air and hotel taxes is the sole responsibility of the winner.
**9.** Void where prohibited by law.

---


## PASSPORT TO ROMANCE VACATION SWEEPSTAKES

# OFFICIAL RULES

**SWEEPSTAKES RULES AND REGULATIONS. NO PURCHASE NECESSARY.**

**HOW TO ENTER:**

**1.** To enter, complete this official entry form and return with your invoice in the envelope provided, or print your name, address, telephone number and age on a plain piece of paper and mail to: Passport to Romance, P.O. Box #1397, Buffalo, N.Y. 14269-1397. No mechanically reproduced entries accepted.
**2.** All entries must be received by the Contest Closing Date, midnight, December 31, 1990 to be eligible.
**3.** Prizes: There will be ten (10) Grand Prizes awarded, each consisting of a choice of a trip for two people to: i) London, England (approximate retail value $5,050 U.S.); ii) England, Wales and Scotland (approximate retail value $6,400 U.S.); iii) Caribbean Cruise (approximate retail value $7,300 U.S.); iv) Hawaii (approximate retail value $ 9,550 U.S.); v) Greek Island Cruise in the Mediterranean (approximate retail value $12,250 U.S.); vi) France (approximate retail value $7,300 U.S.).
**4.** Any winner may choose to receive any trip or a cash alternative prize of $5,000.00 U.S. in lieu of the trip.
**5.** Odds of winning depend on number of entries received.
**6.** A random draw will be made by Nielsen Promotion Services, an independent judging organization on January 29, 1991, in Buffalo, N.Y., at 11:30 a.m. from all eligible entries received on or before the Contest Closing Date. Any Canadian entrants who are selected must correctly answer a time-limited, mathematical skill-testing question in order to win. Quebec residents may submit any litigation respecting the conduct and awarding of a prize in this contest to the Régie des loteries et courses du Quebec.
**7.** Full contest rules may be obtained by sending a stamped, self-addressed envelope to: "Passport to Romance Rules Request", P.O. Box 9998, Saint John, New Brunswick, E2L 4N4.
**8.** Payment of taxes other than air and hotel taxes is the sole responsibility of the winner.
**9.** Void where prohibited by law.


 RLS-DIR

PASSPORT WIN 1 of 10 Vacations SEE INSIDE TO ROMANCE

VACATION SWEEPSTAKES

MONTH 2 ENTRY

# Official Entry Form

Yes, enter me in the drawing for one of ten Vacations-for-Two! If I'm a winner, I'll get my choice of any of the six different destinations being offered — and I won't have to decide until after I'm notified!

Return entries with invoice in envelope provided along with Daily Travel Allowance Voucher. Each book in your shipment has two entry forms — and the more you enter, the better your chance of winning!

Name

Address Apt.

City State/Prov. Zip/Postal Code

Daytime phone number ______________ Area Code

☐ I am enclosing a Daily Travel Allowance Voucher in the amount of $__________ Write in amount revealed beneath scratch-off